GOODBYE, VIETNAM

by Gloria Whelan

Alfred A. Knopf
New York

Whelan

For Patrick

Grateful acknowledgment is made to *Stone Soup, the magazine by children*, for permission to reprint the last two stanzas of "Saigon of Vietnam" by Linh To Sinh My Bui. Copyright © 1990 by the Children's Art Foundation.

This is a Borzoi Book published by Alfred A. Knopf, Inc.

Text copyright © 1992 by Gloria Whelan
Jacket art © 1992 by David Levinson

Library of Congress Cataloging-in-Publication Data
Whelan, Gloria.
   Goodbye, Vietnam / by Gloria Whelan.
      p.   cm.
   Summary: Thirteen-year-old Mai and her family embark on a dangerous sea voyage from Vietnam to Hong Kong to escape the unpredictable and often brutal Vietnamese government.
   ISBN 0-679-82263-1 (trade) — ISBN 0-679-92263-6 (lib. bdg.)
   [1. Refugees—Fiction. 2. Vietnam—Emigration and immigration—Fiction. 3. Sea stories.] I. Title.
PZ7.W5718Wh 1992
[Fic]—dc20   91-3660

Manufactured in the United States of America
10 9 8 7 6 5 4 3 2 1

AUTHOR'S NOTE

I would like to express my gratitude to Tuong Dinh Nguyen, Linh Moran, Vo Van Huyen, Le Thi Dung, and Rose and Allen Pecar.

I would also like to acknowledge the help I received from the Women's Commission for Refugee Women and Children, with special thanks to Diana Bui.

It was dark and cold when the tiny boat
   began to float away from the land of Vietnam.
I didn't want to leave,
but for my future,
I must.

My heart was full of pain when I left.

Oh! My poor country! Whenever can I see you again?
Goodbye Vietnam.
My love country.

     —from "Saigon of Vietnam"
      by Linh To Sinh My Bui, 13,
      Great Falls, Virginia

CONTENTS

PART ONE

The Village

1

I lay in bed listening to the whispering that went on across the room. My world had become a world of whispers, for the frightening things that were happening to us could be spoken of only in whispers. Tonight I could hear the deep, worried whisper of my father, Tran Vinh; the quick, chirping whisper of my mother, Thu; and the grandmother's bossy, rough whisper, which often slid into a whine.

A warm moist breeze found its way through our thatched roof. I rolled over to the edge of the bed, pulling away from the damp touch of my sister, Anh. Anh, who was nine, four years younger than I am, wouldn't go to sleep without holding on to me. My grandmother said it was because Anh was born on *Ty Chap*, the Day of the Mouse. But I knew it was because of Anh's nightmares. The nightmares had started when police had come to our house and threatened to take my grandmother away.

"The old woman is full of dangerous superstition. She pretends to be a healer. She tells fortunes and practices the old religion," they said. "Such things must be wiped out. If we hear she is up to her old tricks, we will take her away and you will never see her again."

When the police left, Anh would not stop crying until my mother promised her, "We will not let anything happen to your grandmother." Since I am older than Anh I knew my mother was making a promise she couldn't keep, for before Anh was born, when I was very young, officers had taken away my father for many months and my mother had not been able to stop them.

In the bed with Anh and me was my six-year-old brother, Thant, who lay curled up like a small animal. Nothing bothers Thant. Because he is the only boy in our family, Thant is spoiled by everyone. Even when there was nothing in the house to eat, my grandmother would sneak Thant some little bit of food she had hidden away. Thant would eat it greedily, never thinking to share it with me and Anh.

The whispers on the other side of the room grew louder. I opened my eyes a little and looked at the three shadowy figures sitting cross-legged on a mat near the altar. The only light came from a small oil lamp that filled the house with smoke and made my eyes smart. It was seldom lighted because oil is so costly. In the days when I went to school I had to hurry to finish my homework while it was still light.

Two years ago I had to stop going to school to work in the rice paddies, for our family needed every penny to keep from starving. My mother was very sad on the day I went to work in the fields. But my grandmother only scoffed at girls who could read. "They will be spoiled for housekeeping, and no man will want them," she said.

My grandmother earned extra money because of her remarkable powers of healing. Of course, she was not an *ong thay phap*, a master of sorcery. That was allowed only to a man and was passed on from father to son. But my grandmother was thought to have much power against evil spirits. She knew all about herbs and the art of letting blood. She even preserved snakes in rice alcohol to make a powerful medicine. My grandmother was also a midwife for the village and had brought many babies into the world. For all these services she received small payments, which she kept hidden, not sharing with us. She had not even helped when my father had been sent away to a camp for nearly a year. There had been nothing to eat then but the frogs we had been able to stick in the fields and a bit of rotted rice.

Listening to the whispering, I could hear talk of my mother's brother, Diep Van Tien, and his family. They had disappeared from our village one night. It was said that they went on a boat and would never come back. Some people in the village were envious of Tien and his family and said they were going to a country where there would be all the food you could eat and no policemen to carry you away. Others disagreed, saying the boats were not an escape but a trick to get your money. Even if you did manage to get on a boat, the boat would not be seaworthy and would sink, or even worse, pirates would descend upon the boat and murder everyone.

But my uncle and his family had been lucky, for many months later my mother received a postcard through the mail. On the back was a picture of a silver city with buildings so many and so tall it was hard to believe the earth could hold them. Neither my father nor my mother can read, so they handed the postcard to me. It was the most important moment of my life. I held the card very carefully and read the message. " 'My honored family: We are now in Hong Kong and soon we go to America to a place called Chicago. We think of you every minute. Make our humble thanks to our ancestors for watching over us.' " It was signed, DIEP VAN TIEN. We were happy for Tien and his family, but we shook our heads over the strange name of the place they were going to.

The card was secretly passed among all the families in the village, and while only Tien and his family had escaped, his freedom gave all of us hope.

The police were angry at the escape of Tien and his family. The whole village suffered. All of our work hours were increased so that we had to leave for the rice fields long before daylight. It was hard work. My back ached from the hours of bending over to push seedlings into the wet mud. Sometimes you worked under the scorching sun. Sometimes the rain poured down on you. Your fingers shriveled from being in the water so long, and when you climbed out of the knee-deep mud your legs were covered with fat, slimy leeches that had to be picked off one by one. The first time Anh helped, she disgraced our whole family by screaming when she discovered the leeches on her legs.

I listened again to the whispers. "Never," I heard

my grandmother hiss in answer to something my father had said. She was so angry she forgot to whisper. "I will die here so that I may lie beside our ancestors. On the sea the *noi* will take all of us."

I trembled. The *noi* were evil spirits that could put a curse on you so strong you would have an irresistible urge to plunge into the water and drown. So awful was the curse, you could drown in something as small as a teacup. I couldn't understand why my grandmother was speaking of the sea. Our village in the Mekong Delta of Vietnam is many miles from the sea. In my geography book I had traced the Mekong River from the Gulf of Siam down to the South China Sea. How large a sea must be, I had thought. The only water I had ever seen besides the water in the fields was the small stream that wound along the edge of our village. But it was so narrow that even my brother Thant with his small chubby arm could fling a stone across it. I could not imagine water that stretched so far you could not see to the other side.

The whispers grew quieter and lulled me to sleep. I woke only briefly when my grandmother pushed her bony frame rudely onto our bed, taking up nearly half the bed's space. My grandmother always smelled of incense and *nuoc mam*, the fish sauce she dabbed on her food. In a minute her quick, sharp little snores began and I fell asleep again, Anh's hand clutching mine for comfort.

When I awoke, my grandmother was already up and burning joss sticks at the altar while she recited her morning prayers. As she kneeled and bent her head to the floor, her sharp elbows stuck out. "She looks like a cricket," Anh giggled in my ear.

It was my job to start the fire for the morning tea. I hurried into my trousers and shirt and went outside to bring in rice stalks and coconut shells to fuel the fire. The pale sunlight was tangled in the branches of the great mango tree that stood in the center of our yard. It was the oldest mango tree in the village and the object of much veneration. My grandmother said its great pools of shade attracted spirits that lounged about under the green canopy. We were forbidden to get too close to the tree lest we interfere with the spirits, but when my grandmother wasn't looking Thant would scramble up the trunk like a monkey and steal the fruit.

In the distance I could see the paddy fields. The last crop of late rice had already been harvested.

Everyone in the village, even Thant, had helped, but there had been no pleasure in our work. The government had come and filled their trucks with the sacks of rice and carried them away. The villagers had grumbled that what was left for us would never last, not even until the hasty rice was harvested in September.

"Hai," my grandmother called to me, "you are slow as a toad this morning."

I hurried in, trying to hold on to the rice stalks that were escaping from my arms and flying about in the light breeze. My mother always called me by my name, Mai, which means "cherry blossom" and which I like. But my grandmother calls me Hai, which means "number-two child." Anh is Ba, or "number-three child." Thant is Tu, or "number-four child." No one is called number-one child. This is a clever trick to confuse the evil spirits that wish to harm young children and that are particularly eager to injure the eldest.

Anh had taken the straw mats from the beds and was airing them. Thant was feeding his two goldfish. My father had brought him the goldfish, and Thant seldom let them out of his sight. The fish, whose names were Yin and Yang, swam about like two slippery orange suns.

For breakfast there were rice balls and tea. It was strong tea because it was the first brewing. Water would be added to the same tea all day. By evening it was hardly worth drinking. My mother served the grandmother first. The grandmother never ate much. This morning she ate almost nothing, putting most of her own portion into Thant's small hand. She was in a cross mood and would not speak a word to anyone. When she finished she went outside with a handful of grain for the two ducks she was raising for the celebration of Tet.

"Why is our grandmother so angry this morning?" Anh asked.

My mother sighed. It would be unbecoming for her to say anything against the mother of her husband, to whom every respect was due, but on this day I could see her heart was as heavy as one of the three stones that lay upon our altar.

"Anh," she said to my sister, "take Thant and help your grandmother round up the ducks." When they were outside, Mother turned to me and spoke in a hushed voice. "You are thirteen now, Mai, and old enough to know what will happen. I am going to tell you something that you must tell to no one else. Our lives will depend on your silence. I am telling you because we will need your help with Anh and Thant when the time comes."

"When the time comes for what?" When I heard the sorrow in my mother's voice, I was not sure I wanted to hear her secret.

"We are going away tomorrow."

"Away?" I said, not understanding.

"We are going to travel to the sea, where we will meet others. A boat will be waiting for us. The boat will take us to Hong Kong. We must go away. The police may come soon to arrest your grandmother because she practices healing and the telling of fortunes. There is almost no food in the village and each day everything costs twice as much as the day before. You are out in the rice fields instead of in school. We must find a better place, but your grandmother does not want to leave the village."

I understood. Everyone wished to stay near the tombs of their ancestors. My family had lived in this village for more than a hundred years. On *Ky*, when the dead are commemorated, people travel great dis-

12

tances to their native villages to honor their ancestors. "Will we come back for *Ky*?" I asked.

"No. We will never come back." My mother hid her face. Now she wept in that silent way she had, so that only the slight shaking of her shoulders and the way her hands covered her face gave away her crying.

I crept closer to her. "But we have no gold," I said. After the Tien family had left the village, it was rumored that nearly nine taels of gold were required to buy their passage.

"A man has come to your father and offered us passage because your father has a skill that is needed." My father's skill was so great a secret that it was not mentioned even now between me and my mother. I knew that under the altar stones there was a hole in the ground. In the hole a metal chest was buried. In the chest were the tools of my father's secret trade. During the war the army of the old government had trained my grandfather as a mechanic. After the war my grandfather taught my father how to use the tools. Soon afterward my grandfather was sent away by the police, and we never heard from him again.

My father pretended to be nothing more than a rice

farmer. If others in the village knew about his secret trade, they said nothing, for everyone had secrets.

"The boat is old," my mother said. "The motor has many infirmities, and a skilled mechanic will be needed to keep it going. A man from a nearby village who knew your grandfather during the time of the war approached us." My mother must have noticed how unhappy I was because she said, "Mai, it is the only way. Even with the harvest, each day we have less and less to eat. And your grandmother is too stubborn to change her ways."

At that moment my grandmother walked into our hut. The two ducks trailed after her, quacking. "The fire is out," she snapped. "The tea will be cold. How is it that two women can sit next to a fire and not see it go out? Why am I cursed with such an idle family? When I die you will be too lazy to put a bowl of rice on the altar for me."

Listening to my grandmother scold my mother, I thought, I'm never going to marry and have the mother of my husband live with me and tell me what to do every minute. "As strict as a husband's mother," people said, and it was true.

2

"Mai," my mother ordered, "take Anh and Thant to the village and buy a little tea at the Chans' store."

Anh and Thant were pleased to be let off their chores. The two of them ran on ahead, balancing themselves on the mud dikes that outlined the paddies. The fields were empty and nearly dry, but in another two months the monsoon would come. The rains would pour down day and night until the ground ran with water and the paddies were flooded again. Everyone would soak their rice seed, and when little pale green sprouts began to uncurl from the split seed, tea and cooked rice would be offered to the spirits to insure a good crop. The seed would be scattered and left to grow until it was high enough to transplant. All summer long the shoots had to be weeded. As they grew, they rippled like green waves in the wind. When the harvesttime drew near, the whole village was fragrant with the smell of the ripening rice.

A narrow footpath running beside the stream led to a dirt road that went into the village. We passed a boy not much older than Thant riding a water buffalo. Thant looked up at the boy enviously. The boy was very proud of his buffalo and would not even look at us. Instead he lay down on the animal's back and stared up into the cloudless sky while the buffalo plodded along, needing no guidance on a road it had taken a thousand times.

When we reached the cemetery where our ancestors are buried, we made our way carefully among the graves to the place where the Tran tomb stood. We were proud of our tombstone. Many graves were marked by nothing more than a mud pile that would wash away in the rains. On some of the graves there were offerings of bits of food to celebrate a death date. With great respect the three of us folded our arms across our bodies and bowed low to our ancestors. Thant in front and Anh and me a little behind him, as befitted girls.

"Grandmother says they're at the altar in our house," Anh said. "How can our ancestors be here and there, too?"

"Maybe they followed us," Thant said.

With a shudder Anh looked quickly about her.

Beyond the cemetery was the temple where you

used to be able to hear the monks saying their prayers, but the government had come and taken the monks away. If the monks had still been there, Thant, when he was a little older, would have gone to join them for several months to practice his religion like a good Buddhist son. He would have had his head shaved and been given an orange robe to wear.

The whole village had been called together and told that the government had closed the temple. My grandmother had muttered under her breath that the temple was the property of the village and that the gods would destroy the government for closing it. My father and mother had tried to hush her, but not before the officers had heard her. Since that time they had never ceased to watch her.

The Chans' store was our favorite place in the village. There were all kinds of things to see and smell: fragrant spices, dried fruits, clouds of mosquito netting, pyramids of straw hats, sweets, woven fish traps, snakelike coils of rope, ceremonial candles, incense, and joss sticks. Many of these things were covered with dust, for few could afford to buy them.

In front of the store were some tables where you could have a bowl of noodles or a cup of tea. One of the tables held household possessions for sale. The villagers brought them in to exchange for food or for a little money.

"Mai." Thant tugged at my arm. "Look, it's our incense burner."

"It can't be," Anh told him. "What would it be doing here?"

"It *is*. Part of its tail is broken off just like ours."

I looked closely at the brass peacock. It did look like the one that had stood on our altar as long as I could remember. Next to the incense burner was something else that looked familiar: a white china offering plate with a border of blue chrysanthemums. I knew it must be ours because right in the middle of the plate was a picture of a dragonfly. Thant was pointing a finger at some ebony chopsticks. There were four pairs bound together by a bit of red ribbon. They were the chopsticks our mother brought out when company came.

"There are your teeth marks, Thant," Anh said. Once when Thant was very young he had grabbed one and chewed on it. Our father had wanted to punish him, for the chopsticks had been passed down from one generation to another, but our grandmother had

18

said it was a good sign and showed that Thant would eat well all of his life.

Our possessions seemed to be scattered about on the table: rice bowls, our best cooking pot, the kerosene can, our father's sickle, our mother's green silk sash with the small tear that she had carefully mended. Anh and Thant wanted to ask the Chans where they had gotten all of our things, but I made them wait outside while I went in to get the tea.

I wanted to tell Anh and Thant the secret of our leaving, but I had given my word. I thought our parents must be desperate in their need to get money for the trip; otherwise they would not have risked selling things that might be recognized by our neighbors, who would surely guess we were planning to leave. I felt sadder than ever, for when my mother told me we were leaving I hadn't realized everything we owned would have to stay behind and that all the familiar bits and pieces that went to make up our life would disappear.

On our return we saw our father standing at the doorway. We ran down the path toward him, scattering the ducks. I thought our father had never looked so sad, not even when the police had taken him away to the camp for a year. Inside the house we could hear the wailing of our grandmother and the soft hushing noises of our mother.

Thant grabbed at our father's leg. "Why are all our things at the Chans'? Are we going to get new ones?"

Father frowned. "Where did you see them?"

"On the table in front of the store," Anh told him.

Father hurried us inside. Calling to Mother, he said, "Chan has our things out for everyone to see. You said he promised to wait until tomorrow."

"What can it matter?" Our mother sighed. "No one in the village would be so cruel as to give us away. In a few hours we will be gone."

"You told me we wouldn't leave until tomorrow," I said.

Anh stared at me. "You knew something and didn't tell us."

"It wasn't Mai's fault," my mother said. "I made her promise not to tell."

"But why *tonight*?" I insisted.

"We have heard that the officers are coming tomorrow for your grandmother," Father said. "Listen carefully. As soon as it is dark, we will leave the village and take the road to Go Cong. We must travel by night. It will be a hard trip and a dangerous one. We can carry only a few things. At Go Cong there will be a boat. I will have charge of the engine."

"When will we come back?" Anh asked.

At that our grandmother began to wail again. "Who will tend the tomb of your father and grandfather and great-grandfather? Leave me behind," she begged. "I'm too old to go to some barbarian land. Leave me here to die in peace."

"We cannot leave you behind. Part of the reason for our going is the danger you are in. I am your oldest son and you must obey me."

Muttering, our grandmother began to gather together the little envelopes of paper and the small bottles and boxes in which she kept her herbal medicines. She looked at no one. Even Thant could not catch her eye. I saw how old our grandmother had grown. Her skin was darkened and shriveled like the husk of a coconut from years of work in the fields. Her shoulder blades showed through her shirt, sharp as two knives. She was hard and spare like a pebble worn small and thin by a stream.

After checking carefully up and down the path to be sure no one was in sight, our father removed the altar stones and began to scoop away the soft dirt of the floor. In a few minutes he had uncovered a metal chest. He opened it and looked proudly at the tools that lay neatly arranged inside. "These are our passage on the boat," he said.

We needed to take water with us, so I was sent out to the large brick tank to bring in rainwater. I carried a bit of netting with me to strain the mosquito larva out of the pail. There had been almost no rain, and I had to lean down into the tank to get what little water remained. In another week it would be gone and we would have to carry water all the way from the well in the village. I caught myself. Only we would not be here.

Leaning down into the dark water tank was frightening. Suppose a *ma da* should be lurking there, I thought. The *ma da* were the ghosts of the drowned who could not rest in peace until they had lured someone else to perish in the water to take their place. Children were the *ma da*'s favorite victims. My grandmother told terrible stories of how the ghosts float over the water wailing, "It is cold, so cold." I hurried into our hut, nearly upsetting the pail. If I was afraid of a rainwater tank, I thought, what was it going to be like with the great sea all around us?

When the darkness came, our father ordered everyone to join him at the family altar. Reverently he lighted the joss sticks. Our grandmother handed him offerings of rice and the tea I had bought to place on the altar. We all fell to our knees and kowtowed. In a hushed voice our father explained to our ancestors why it was necessary for the family to leave our home and our altar. "If we do not go, my children will come of age without their grandmother and their father. There is no one to teach my son his religious duties. In the schools the children learn to disobey their parents. The dead are no longer honored. We ask that you forgive us and when we make a suitable home for you in some far country, that you will come to us and take your rightful place at our new altar."

We kowtowed once more, and our father told us to take up our baskets. But it was many minutes before we could bring ourselves to do as he asked.

Our grandmother was the last to leave the house, the house of her son, her husband's house, and the house of her husband's father. The basket she carried was so large it tilted her whole body to one side. "You're taking too much," my father complained. "What do you have in there?"

"There is nothing in the basket but a few clothes and my medicines. Would you deprive me of those?"

Thant was taking double steps to keep up with our father. Our mother and Anh walked hand in hand. I was left to walk beside the grandmother, who grumbled and scolded under her breath. Once I paused to look back over my shoulder for a last glimpse of our house. It seemed to me that the whole family was still back there drinking their evening tea, while the six people who hurried along the path were no more than moon shadows that would disappear with the first cloud. Leaving the house forever made me feel like a turtle that had climbed out of its shell. Anything might hurt me.

Our grandmother yanked at my sleeve to hurry me along. A quacking sound came from her basket. It was the two Tet ducks. The rest of the family was too far ahead to have heard the ducks. My grandmother reached over and pinched me to let me know I was to say nothing. I grinned. It was two things less to leave behind.

PART TWO

The Journey

3

"Our journey to Go Cong will take us two nights of walking," our father said. "We have no papers from the government giving us permission to leave our village, so we must travel when it is dark."

At first we kept to the road, where the walking was not difficult, but just before daylight an army jeep rumbled over the crest of a hill. "Quickly!" My father led us into the brush, where it was swampy. We sunk to our knees in muck.

"Are there snakes?" Anh whispered before my mother put a hand over her mouth.

The beams from the headlights of the jeep touched the trees we were crouching behind. I heard the soldiers' laughter and saw the glow from their cigarettes. Anh was holding on to me so tightly I could hardly breathe. Only minutes after the soldiers passed by, the ducks popped out of our grandmother's basket and began quacking.

My father was furious. "How could you be so foolish as to carry those ducks with you?" he demanded of my grandmother. "If that had happened when the jeep was passing we would have been captured. Get rid of those fool ducks at once!"

My grandmother sat down on the road next to her basket. "If they cannot come, neither will I."

"Then stay." My father led us away. We kept looking over our shoulders at the grandmother, who was sitting with her basket where we had left her. As the distance grew, she became smaller and smaller. Thant and Anh began to cry. At last my father cursed under his breath and motioned to her. She picked up her basket and with no great speed joined us. "If I hear one more sound from those birds, we will kill them on the spot," he warned her, but no one believed him.

As soon as the sky lightened and the sun began to rise, our father led us deeper into the swampy ground. Thant stumbled over the fallen trees and Anh was half asleep. I had stopped thinking about anything but moving one foot after the other. Each step we took sent up a cloud of hungry mosquitoes. We finally came to a rise in the ground where we could huddle together and keep dry. All around us grew strange plants with huge green leaves. The roots of the trees stuck out of the water like large crooked hands. Birds called from the tops of the trees with unfamiliar songs to warn one another of our coming.

The dampness and the heat made us listless. No one wanted more than a few bites of the rice cakes our mother handed out. All day long we dozed off and on, waking to slap at a mosquito or to move into a bit of shade. I had a blister on my foot from the long walk. I did not know if I could walk much farther, but as soon as the sun set, our father hurried us out of the swamp.

Father swung Thant up on his shoulders, and I had to half drag Anh along with me. Mother was carrying both her own and our grandmother's basket. Just when I wanted nothing more than to sink down on the ground, not caring whether the soldiers found us or not, we came up over the crest of a hill and there before us were the lights of Go Cong. "They look like fireflies," Anh whispered. We all stood still, awed by the sight of such a large city.

Now we were much less safe. The swamp and brush had fallen away. It was all open country. Small lakes and acres of paddies lay on either side of us. If soldiers came along there would be no place to run for protection. We hurried, but our father urged us to go even faster. "We must get to the town before day-light." Several times he took a scrap of paper from his pocket to memorize the drawing of the house of the man who would lead us to the boat. To ask directions in the city would be to draw attention to ourselves as outsiders.

It was early morning when we reached the out-skirts of the town. A shopkeeper was opening the shutters of his store to prepare for business. We could see that his shelves were nearly empty. From one of the street corners an officer watched suspiciously. Bi-cyclers passed on their way to work. I stayed as close to my parents as I could. Even our grandmother walked in my father's shadow. I was disappointed at how shabby everything was.

Father cautioned us to keep our eyes on the ground and not to gawk like country people. As we wandered through the narrow streets, he consulted his bit of paper. He was guiding us toward a house when a policeman blocked our way.

"Where are your papers?" the officer demanded. He was thin and looked as though he had been on duty for many hours and still had many more hours to go. If father had shown our papers, the officer would have known we came from a distant village. He would have been suspicious.

"We live just outside the town," my father said. "We are paying a visit to my cousin, who is ill. We were upset when we heard of the illness and did not think to bring our papers."

"What do you have there?" The officer reached out for the basket that held my father's tools. Not only were such tools forbidden, but if they were discovered, they would be taken away. Then there would be no place for us on the boat.

With a quick shove, my grandmother pushed her way in front of my father, giving the officer a sly grin. "Our relative, who is dear to us, is very sick, and we are bringing him nourishment to make him strong." She pulled back the cover from her basket and the ducks thrust their heads up and looked about with wild, beady eyes. "It is possible that one duck might serve to feed him," she said, "in which case this second duck might not be needed."

The officer looked longingly at the ducks and then over his shoulder. There was no one else on the street. His hand reached out and grabbed one of the ducks around its neck and snatched it out of the basket. So great a look of pleasure came over the officer's face, the duck might already be in his pot cooking instead of flapping about in his hands. He stuffed the bird inside his jacket and turned on his heel. As he walked briskly away, we could see the legs of the duck dangling out of his jacket.

"The ducks you wanted me to leave behind," my grandmother said smugly, "have saved our lives."

4

Father said, "Quickly, it is the house with the banana tree." It was a poor-looking house with a few scrawny chickens scratching in the yard. No sooner had we started up the path than the door opened wide like a mouth hungry for food. We were hurried along by a man who called himself Quach Loc. His wife stood next to him. They looked more like brother and sister than husband and wife. Both were short and plump with round faces and pudgy, dimpled little hands. "Come in." Quach Loc rushed us through the door, which he hastily shut. "You are the Vinh family? You have brought your tools?"

My father opened his chest, proudly displaying what was inside. The man nodded his approval. "Your boat is owned by Captain Muoi. I am sure there will be no trouble. It will be a pleasure trip. You must buy your food for the journey. I know a place where it can be had with no questions asked. I will go with you. First you must all have a cup of tea." Loc indicated that we should be seated.

We dropped our baskets with relief and sank down onto the floor mats. The man appeared friendly, but he smiled too much. I began to be afraid.

"I believed the food would be provided," my father said.

"Provided! No, indeed. You are lucky to have a passage on the boat. *Provided!* Some people are never satisfied. But my wife will provide you with tea. Yes, indeed. Quach Loc knows how to be hospitable."

While the tea was being poured out, I glanced quickly about the room and saw that a woman and a girl were sitting in the shadows. The girl was about my age and was wearing American blue jeans. I knew what they were because I had once seen a boy come through our village in the dark blue trousers.

Quach Loc called to the woman, "*Bac si* Hong, you and your daughter Kim must join us." We were surprised, for *bac si* is a title that indicates honor is due the person. Loc turned to us and in a low voice said, "*Bac si* Hong is a doctor. It is very strange to call a woman *bac si*."

I saw that the doctor lady disliked the fat little man. The girl, Kim, moved shyly to her mother's side and hung on to her mother's hand. They seated themselves a little apart from us. I knew it was rude, but I couldn't help staring at the woman. I had never seen a doctor before. A doctor who was a woman seemed almost unimaginable.

Quach Loc whispered to us, "*Bac si* Hong has had a most sad time. Her husband, who was once a well-known university professor in Ho Chi Minh City, was taken away by the police. Only last month he returned a sick man and died. *Bac si* Hong and her daughter will be on the boat with you."

Bac si Hong and Kim did not drink their tea. Their faces were empty of expression. I saw that both the mother and daughter had squares of white material pinned to their clothes to let others know they were in mourning. I looked hastily away, but Thant could not take his eyes off the two strangers. He inched his way to the *bac si*, who was very beautiful, and touched the soft material of her skirt. My mother was horrified at this rudeness and pulled him back, but the *bac si* had come to life and reached out for Thant's hand.

Our grandmother was frowning at the *bac si*. We had heard the grandmother scoff at doctors, because they had to go to school to learn to heal. "You cannot buy such knowledge," she always said. "It must be passed down from one sorcerer to another."

Our father excused himself. "If food is needed, I had better go and find it. We thank you for your tea."

Quach Loc followed him. "I am known here, and the storekeepers will give you a better bargain when they see you are my friend."

We all waited silently for my father and Quach Loc to return. Our mother and grandmother didn't take their eyes from the door, but Thant and Anh fell asleep, Thant with his head on my mother's lap, Anh sitting against the wall, one hand holding on to me. I sometimes thought Anh was as much a part of me as my arm or leg.

I wanted to move closer to the girl, Kim, and maybe even talk with her. Ho Chi Minh City was a huge place. Much, much bigger than even Go Cong. I wondered what it would be like to live in such a city. I had a thousand questions to ask, but I didn't want to awaken Anh by moving and I couldn't catch the girl's eye. Before I knew it my eyes fluttered shut and I was asleep.

When I awoke, my father had returned and was talking in a quick, hushed whisper to my mother. "It took all of our money," he was saying, "and I know that thief Quach Loc got a commission on everything I bought." He looked hastily in the direction of the kitchen, where Loc and his wife were also whispering together, but the look on their faces was one of satisfaction.

The man who was to take us to the boat arrived only moments after it grew dark. He was a small man with a crafty face like a monkey's. Quach Loc introduced us. The man consulted a paper he held and, bowing before *Bac si* Hong, said, "From you, eight taels of gold for yourself and your daughter."

I caught my breath. So much money! There was not that much in all of our village.

Bac si Hong reached into a canvas bag and took out a leather purse. One by one she placed the small gold coins into the man's outstretched hand. As she was counting out the money, the man was staring at her hand. When she had finished he said, "Now I must ask for one tael to give as a bribe to the officers who guard the harbor."

Bac si Hong raised her eyes and stared hopelessly at the man. "That is all I have," she said. "We had to sell everything to get that much." She held out the leather purse. "Look for yourself."

"I will take your ring," he said, pointing to a wide gold band on her left hand.

"But that is my wedding ring."

The man shrugged. "If you don't wish to go . . . ?"

Bac si Hong began to tug at her ring. "I can't give it to you," she said. "It hasn't been off for years."

"Allow me," he said. He grabbed her hand and began to twist the ring, but it would not come off. In disgust the man gave up. "What else do you have?" He snatched at her bag and emptied it onto the floor. Pushing aside a small heap of clothes, he took up a leather case. "What is in here?"

"Medicines," she answered. "There may be sickness on the boat."

"Medicine is scarce and sells well. I'll accept it in payment."

"Wait," *Bac si* Hong said. "There is something of my daughter's I could give you instead of the medicines." I saw her give Kim a pleading look. "The medicines may save lives, Kim," she said.

When Kim did not move, her mother reached over and took from her hand a long black case, which she opened. Inside was a thin silver object.

"What is it?" the little man asked greedily. He reached for it, but Kim pulled it out of her mother's hand.

"It's a flute," she said, and lifted the instrument to her lips. She began to make the strangest, most beautiful music I had ever heard.

The man dropped his hand and stood staring at Kim while she played. The music sounded to me as if it ought to be played in pleasant gardens where there were fountains. When Kim finished, she put the flute back into its case and handed it to the man. He shook his head, indicating that she should keep it. But he was embarrassed by being caught in a kind act, and when he turned away, his voice was rough. "Come with me," he ordered.

Quach Loc opened the door for us. He and his wife bowed low in farewell. Our family, with Kim and her mother, followed the little man. I had not liked the house of Quach Loc, but it seemed safer to me than the unknown streets of Go Cong.

5

The man led us through the darkened city toward the harbor. Our father walked ahead. Our mother followed with Thant holding her hand. It was rare for Thant to allow anyone to take his hand. Anh and I came next and behind us the grandmother and *Bac si* Hong with Kim. We were silent as we walked through the dark streets. Soon I smelled something strange. Although I had never smelled it before, I knew what it was. The sea. We were at the harbor. I could make out the shapes of sampans with their shrimplike tails curled over the backs of the boats. The lanterns that hung from the masts looked like they were floating in the air. The man had stopped. Ahead of us on a wharf a crowd of people huddled together. As we came closer, the knot of people pushed and shoved against us. I pulled back. When I had thought about the trip I had thought about being on the boat with my family. Then I had added Kim and her mother, thinking I would be glad for Kim's company if Kim would just look at me or speak to me. Of course, I knew all along there would be other people on the boat, but I had never expected this many. "Is it a very large boat?" I asked.

"The boat is no more than forty feet," my father answered. "All these people will not fit on such a boat."

"But haven't they paid their passage?" asked our mother. "They cannot be left behind!"

"If they are, who will they complain to?" said our father. "People are put in jail for trying to leave the country."

"But they will have no money left for another boat," I said.

"No," our father replied gravely.

The little man had disappeared into the cabin of the boat. Now he came in search of our father. "You are to come aboard," he said to Father. "The boat must leave before it is discovered, but the engine won't cooperate. If you can't do something with it in a hurry, there will be no trip." The people around us heard the man's words and quickly repeated them. A silence fell over the crowd.

"My family must be allowed to come with me," Father said.

The man nodded. The people knew what my father was wanted for and drew aside to allow us to pass. As I hurried after my parents, I saw the frightened look on Kim's face. Without thinking of what I was doing, I reached out and grabbed Kim's hand, pulling her with us. Kim's mother understood. She picked up their bundles and hurried after our family. A man guarding the entrance to the boat pointed to Kim and *Bac si* Hong. "Who are they?" he asked me.

I don't know where I found the courage, but I said, "My aunt and my cousin."

"Well, move quickly," he said.

Leading to the boat was a gangplank so narrow there was room for only one person at a time. A lantern illuminated the boat. I thought there must be some mistake—the boat was so small. How, I wondered, would all those people on the wharf fit into it? The boat looked very old, as though it had been floating on the sea for many years.

The man told us to stay where we were and went off with my father. For the first time Kim's mother spoke. "They are no better than murderers to send us off in such a boat. The first wave will crush it." She looked in the direction of the wharf as though she were considering making her way back with Kim. A moment later the anger disappeared and the look of despair that had been on her face since we had first seen her returned.

Our grandmother was sobbing. "We will all drown," she wailed. "The *ma da* will reach out of the water and pull the boat down to the bottom of the sea. We will drown and our spirits will never rest."

My mother tried to comfort her, but the wailing continued. Thant and Anh began to cry. I felt tears in my own eyes and saw that Kim had buried her face against her mother. *Bac si* Hong looked at us and gently pushed Kim away. "Crying will not help." Her voice was suddenly businesslike. "We must find a good place for ourselves before the others come." She looked quickly about the boat. There was a small cabin made of planks that looked as if they did not quite fit together. Inside the cabin was the entrance to the lower part of the boat where my father had been taken to work on the engine.

"Perhaps we should go down below," my mother suggested. I knew she wanted to be close to my father. I agreed. I didn't want to look at all that sea. My grandmother began to move toward the small cabin but Kim's mother stopped her.

"No, the air in the hold will be stale and close. There are sure to be rats, perhaps carrying disease. Should anything happen to the boat, we would be trapped. The best place to be is where the food is prepared. That way we will be among the first to be served. Kim, you and Mai see if you can help me find the stove."

I followed Kim, not really wanting to go. I kept looking back over my shoulder so I could make out the shapes of my mother and grandmother. It was dark and we had to move slowly, feeling our way as we went. I had never been on a boat, and the rolling motion felt funny. You put a foot where you thought something solid was but nothing was there to meet you. I could hear the sound of the small waves slapping against the boat, letting us know the water was out there. I tripped over a broken plank in the deck and bumped my head.

"Mai," Kim called to me, "look."

When I found her, Kim placed my hands on a large metal can. It was warm to the touch. We could see a grill on top and red embers inside. We called out to the others that we had found the stove.

Kim's mother was pleased. "Good, we will make a place for ourselves here."

There was a sound of sputterings and deep coughs from the engine. "Hurry," Kim's mother called. "Spread out your things to mark your place. Once the engine starts they will herd everyone aboard and cast off so as not to waste fuel."

My mother seemed unsure. "It will be better to wait for my husband to choose a place for us."

But Kim's mother had already begun to settle into the spot she had chosen. I had never heard a woman give orders except my grandmother, and those were always given in a whining voice, not as a man gives orders. Still, everything Kim's mother said made sense. I decided to arrange our things as well.

The sounds of the engine grew stronger, stopped, started again, wheezed, stopped. A long silence and then the whole boat shook with the sound of the engine. There were cheers from the shore and excited shouts from the crowd as they all tried to rush up the narrow gangplank at once. As people poured onto the deck, they were herded into the hold.

"Why are they making them go down there?" my

mother asked, worrying that we had made the wrong choice.

"If everyone stays on deck the boat will be unstable," Kim's mother said. "People are needed in the hold as ballast. Besides, all the people would not fit on the deck. Now we must be very quiet so we are not made to go below. Once the hold is full, we will be safe."

The people onshore were desperate to get on deck and would not stop pushing. Suddenly there was a splash, followed by shouts. "My husband!" someone was screaming. "My husband has fallen into the water!" For a moment there was silence, and the movement of the crowd seemed to come to a halt. Then it began again and the woman's screams were lost in the rush of people crowding onto the boat.

Although I could no longer hear the screams, they echoed back and forth inside my head. I would have run from the boat, but people were pushing in against us from all sides, trying to find a bit of space. Our own space became smaller and smaller. "Lie down," Kim's mother told us. We lay down on the deck, hoping to keep enough room so we could stretch out at night and sleep, but it was no use. There were too many people. I felt someone sitting on my legs and quickly drew them up, losing the little extra space I had. Someone stepped on Thant. He cried out, and when my mother picked him up to comfort him, Thant's space was lost to us. Soon we were huddled together with barely enough room to move our arms. Still the people came. I felt the breath and smelled the smell of strangers all around me.

The boat had been rocking gently. Now the engine gave a great wheeze, and I felt a lurch as the boat moved away from the wharf and made its way out into the harbor. There were terrible cries from those on the wharf left behind. Once the boat began to move, the jostling for space stopped. The movement of the small ship out into the darkness of the sea silenced everyone. We all held our breath, waiting.

Anh said, "Will the sea stop after a while? Will we fall over the edge?"

"No," I told her. "There is land on the other side of the sea." I tried to recall the picture on the post-card the Tien family had sent from the silver city. I heard my grandmother whispering to the duck, trying to quiet it. I knew from Thant's light breathing that he was already asleep. The sound of the engine told me my father was watching over the boat. I felt my eyes close.

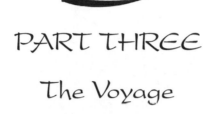

PART THREE

The Voyage

6

When I opened my eyes it was morning. My legs were cramped from being drawn up all night into so small a space. My hair and clothes felt damp and clammy. It was only a morning sun, but the light danced on the water and the heat felt like the middle of the afternoon. I looked around me. The boat was crowded with awakening people: old people, families with children, young men, people who were traveling alone, people who looked as if they came from the country, as we had, and city people like Kim and *Bac si* Hong. The boat was like a small, crowded village coming to life. In a few places where someone had edged into someone else's space, polite arguments were going on. People were tying their straw hats on against the sun. Some had little tins of water and were washing themselves. A man was going about collecting from each passenger some rice to be boiled. Babies were crying. Some were being nursed. My grandmother and an old man were standing side by side watching the outline of the land grow fainter and fainter. I tried to guess at the number of passengers. Forty or fifty, I decided. It was hard to believe that with so many passengers the small boat could stay afloat.

Our father was trying to make his way toward us. With every step he took people had to pull in their legs or shift their body to make room for him to get by. My mother was standing up waiting for him. He took her hand. I had never seen my parents touch in public. My father rested his hand for a moment on each of us—Thant first, then Anh and me, and even our grandmother—as though he could not believe we were actually there in the boat until he had touched us. He nodded politely to Kim and her mother, embarrassed that they should see him show so much emotion. "It will be a wonder if the engine continues to run," he grumbled. "It must be the first engine that was ever made, and the boat timbers are rotted and waterlogged. What's more, the man who owns the boat, Captain Muoi, is a fool. This is the only map he has." Father showed us a page torn from a book. I recognized our country and the South China Sea, even though their names were written in a strange language.

"It must be from an English geography book," Kim said. "My mother taught me English."

My grandmother looked at the strange printing, then at Kim as though she were a witch.

A voice boomed out over our heads. Looming above us was the biggest man I had ever seen in my life. He was like a great thick banyan tree. He wore an old cap pushed back on his head with bits of tarnished gold braid stuck here and there. Beneath his cap I could see his head had been shaved. Although he did not appear old, his tanned face was crosshatched with wrinkles. He looked happy, as though he had something pleasant to tell us. "You are the most fortunate people on earth!" he shouted. "You are under the care of Captain Muoi and you are sailing on the finest ship in the China Sea. You must remember that I am your father while you are on my ship. We will all be one happy family. What belongs to one of us belongs to all. If you hoard food and do not turn it over to our cook, Le Hung, you will be a bad child and your father Captain Muoi will have to punish you." He pointed an accusing finger at a woman who was washing her baby's face and hands with a rag dipped in a small bowl of water. "There will be no washing with the drinking water. Our journey is a thousand miles, and water will be more precious to us than gold. It is only for drinking. A small ration will be given out in the morning to each family. If you are good and obedient children you will find me the kindest father in the world. If not, we feed you to the fishes!" His shoulders heaved as he laughed at his wit. Then he stooped low to clear the cabin door and disappeared inside.

"Has he made the trip to Hong Kong before?" Kim's mother asked my father.

"I don't think he's ever done anything in this boat but carry black market goods up and down the coast. I think he knows nothing about navigating on the sea." My father saw our worried faces. "Never mind," he assured us. "We'll get there safely in spite of Muoi. Now I must go back. The engine needs constant watching."

The passengers busied themselves with arranging their tiny living space. Mats were unrolled and laid on the deck. Other mats and bits of clothing were supported on sticks to make sun shades. My grandmother was secretly feeding a bit of rice to the duck.

She had already argued with Le Hung, when he had come to collect our food. He was eager to take the duck. "Before I was put in prison for talking too much I was a cook in a restaurant in a town that would swallow ten of your villages," he said. "I know how a duck should be cooked."

The grandmother insisted the duck must be saved for the celebration of Tet, which was still many days away. "Can't you see? The duck is a member of our family," she told him.

Le Hung laughed loudly at that. He danced lightly across the sprawled bodies on the deck, joking with everyone. He was happy to have escaped.

Bac si Hong saw that our mother was shy in the presence of so many strangers and tried to make her more comfortable by asking her about our village. At first our mother was embarrassed to be speaking with a *bac si*, who was educated, but after a while she forgot her embarrassment in the pleasure of speaking about our village. Speaking of it brought it closer.

I did not want to talk of the village. I was eager to learn from Kim what Ho Chi Minh City was like. "What did you do in the city?" I asked her. "Are there movies there?" I had heard of such things.

"Yes," Kim said. "Sometimes we would go to the movies or to a restaurant for dinner. Or we would just walk along the boulevards. But that was before my father died." She looked away. I saw that there were as many sorrows in the city as there were in the country.

The motion of the boat changed. Instead of the gentle roll that had lulled me to sleep the night before, now the boat pitched and tossed as though it were climbing a hill only to fall down the other side. Anh began to whimper. "My stomach feels funny," she told our mother. She was not the only one.

An old man who sat on the other side of my mother had bowed to us and introduced himself as Pham Van Quang. "This is my son, Pham Van Tho, and Dao, the wife of my son," he said. Dao sat quietly with all their possessions heaped around her as though she were eager to hide a fact that could not be hidden. She was soon going to have a baby.

Quang was looking anxiously at his daughter-in-law Dao, whose face was pale and whose arms were wrapped tightly about her body. From time to time she made little moaning noises. The old man apologized to us. "It is the rolling of the boat now that we are out at sea." He added softly, "And her condition."

Late in the afternoon we watched Le Hung start a fire in the oil drum that he used as a stove. A big pot of rice was put on to boil. Cheers went up. Most of the passengers had not eaten in more than a day.

But when Hung threw large handfuls of green kale into a pan and the strong smell of the kale spread over the deck, the passengers began stumbling over one another on their way to lean over the sides of the boat. The sound of their retching sickened others and soon half the passengers were crowded at the railing.

Captain Muoi shouted, "Hung, they haven't even tasted your dinner and already they are ill. You will save us a lot of food." His loud laughter only made the sick passengers feel worse.

Dao made two trips to the boat's railing. Anh had gone once with our mother. I found that if I sat very still and thought hard about something besides food I could keep myself from being sick. Kim's mother was handing out pills. She offered one to my mother and to Anh. "This will take away the sickness," she explained. Our grandmother snatched the pill from Mother and held it in her hand, studying it. I knew she was embarrassed not to have her own remedy to offer. But our village was far from the sea and there had been no need for the grandmother to cure such an illness.

After turning the small pill about in her hand, regarding it all the while with great suspicion, she gave it to my mother. "You may take it," she said, "but it is doubtful that there is any power in it. I would put together some of my own medicines, but this seasickness is a small thing and not worth my time."

"You are a healer?" Kim's mother asked.

"She's the best one in our village," I answered proudly.

"Then we are in the same profession," *Bac si* Hong told my grandmother. My grandmother looked to see if the *bac si* was poking fun at her, but Kim's mother was only trying to be friendly. My grandmother bowed.

All day long the sun beat down on us. The men took off their shirts and rolled up their trousers. The women wore as little as was decent. Any breeze that blew was like the fiery breath of a dragon. People were too hot to move. We wore our straw hats, but the sun glanced off the water and came at us from all sides. The water ration was small, and we were always thirsty. Old Pham Van Quang gave much of his water ration to his daughter-in-law Dao. The grandmother coaxed Le Hung to give her a bit of extra water for the duck with the promise that on Tet he would have a share of the meat.

The few clothes we wore were stained with sweat and stuck to our bodies. The sea spray dried on our skin, leaving a sticky white crust. Worst of all was the crowding. You could not stick out your legs or arms without bumping into someone else. If you tried to move to another part of the boat it was nearly impossible not to step on someone. When you stood up, your legs were so cramped and weak from not being used, they hardly supported you.

At first people spoke only to members of their families or to those who were huddled next to them. But the seasickness brought us closer. You could not stumble back and forth to the railing of the boat without making many apologies. There were words of sympathy between mothers whose children were ill, and there was good-natured joking among the men, who taunted one another for being seasick.

Everyone had tales of misery to exchange: sons and

husbands sent off and never seen again, houses and lands taken by the government. For the first time these things could be spoken aloud. For the first time there was no one to fear. Even if the voyage was dangerous and uncomfortable, even if we were crowded together in a tiny rotting boat in the middle of the sea with little water and food and a crazy captain, at least we could speak our thoughts aloud.

Although it tempted the spirits to take our safety for granted, we could not help talking of the good things that would be ahead for us. Mother showed the postcard that our uncle Tien had sent from Hong Kong, and everyone exclaimed at the beauty and size of the city. It was known that even if we all survived the voyage, refugees were not always welcome in Hong Kong, but we told ourselves if we traveled so far and sacrificed so much they must take us in. From Hong Kong it was thought possible to move to other countries. Some of the passengers boasted of relatives in Australia and Europe and even America, where Uncle Tien had hoped to go. Scraps of paper with the names and addresses of relatives in these strange-sounding places were proudly displayed.

"Would you want to go to America?" I asked Kim. It seemed so far.

"Yes, only we don't know anyone there. But we speak English. That may help."

I thought of a country where everyone went about in the handsome blue jeans that Kim wore. "Would you teach me English?" I asked.

I learned from Kim the English words you use for greeting people and words for getting food. The strange words sounded flat and unmusical.

My grandmother did not like my learning English words. She complained to my mother that such knowledge was foolishness and dangerous besides, but my mother was too worried about Anh to listen to the grandmother's grumblings.

Anh, who always had so much to say, had grown silent and tearful. She hung on to me and to my mother as well. *Bac si* Hong examined Anh, much to my grandmother's disgust. "Physically, I can find nothing wrong with her," Kim's mother said. "Perhaps too much has happened these last few days and she doesn't know what to make of it all."

It was not until early evening and the hot sun was

burning low on the horizon like a great fire and Kim played her flute that Anh seemed herself again. I think it was the flute. Its sound was like the ringing of silver bells or cool water poured out of a clear glass. No one on the boat spoke while Kim played. After the music ended, people lay down quietly, ready for sleep.

Lying there squeezed into as small a shape as possible, I thought about Kim's music. I had never heard such sounds. They were a puzzle. How could something speak to you so well without words? Then I thought, There are many things that do that: the fragrance of rice when you knew the harvest was near, the taste of ripe mangoes from the tree in our yard. For some things words were not needed.

The next day there were many sick passengers. An old couple from the city, unused to the heat, developed bad cases of sunstroke. There was dysentery, and the tiny space at the back of the boat, curtained off for a toilet, was always in use. Kim's mother had ordered the drinking water boiled, but no one paid attention to her order. It was too much trouble, Le Hung said, and there was not enough fuel for the stove. *Bac si* Hong told us to drink nothing but tea.

Some of the sick people came to Kim's mother, who gave them medicine. Some asked my grandmother to help them. Kim watched open-mouthed as the grandmother made small cuts on the back of one sick man and put little rubber cups on the cuts to take some of the blood. I had often seen my grandmother treat sick people in that way and thought nothing of it.

Every hour or two Captain Muoi popped out of the cabin. "You are lucky people," he would tell us. "Yesterday we made excellent time. It is only a matter of a few days before we reach Hong Kong. You are fortunate to be in the capable hands of Captain Muoi."

I knew from our father, who joined us for our morning and evening meals, that things were not going as well as Captain Muoi said. The engine had broken down twice. Without power we drifted for hours. Afterward there had been arguments as to our course. Some said the captain's compass was not working and we were going in the wrong direction.

My father carried Thant off with him to keep him company while he worked on the engine. "It is not too soon to learn a trade for our new country," he told Thant. When Thant returned he had grease on his face and hands and Captain Muoi's hat on his head, and he boasted of how the captain let him steer the boat.

"Ha," said Quang, "a six-year-old can do a better job than that fool captain."

To pass the time I begged Kim to tell me about the movies. Kim said she had seen lots of movies with American cowboys on horses. You did not even have to go to the movies to see such things, she said. "We had a television set right in our own house, and you could turn it on and see things that were happening all over the world."

That seemed a magic beyond believing to me. "Where is the television set now?" I asked. I was sorry she had not brought it with her.

"That was five years ago," she said, "before my father was taken away. He taught at a university, but he would not teach what the government wanted him to, and he was sent to work in the fields. He wasn't used to such work and he became very sick. They sent him home, but my mother's medicines couldn't help him and he died." When Kim finished her story she took up her flute and played such sad music that even Captain Muoi, who had come out to make one of his cheerful speeches, stood half bent over in the cabin door staring at Kim. When the music ended he went back into the cabin without saying a word.

7

At the start of our voyage the grandmother had cast a horoscope for Dao's baby, naming two auspicious days for its birth. When the first lucky day went by and the baby didn't come, Quang shook his head in disappointment, but on the second auspicious day Dao started making sharp little grunting noises and Quang became hopeful. By late afternoon Dao's little grunts became louder. Sweat poured down her face. She held on to her husband Tho's hand, and Tho gave her little sips of water. My mother had borrowed clothing to make a curtained area around Dao. Everyone was excited at the thought of a baby being born on our boat. Everyone except Captain Muoi. The captain told Tho, "If I had known the baby was expected so soon, you would never have been allowed on board my ship."

It was suppertime before the baby decided to be born. I had been home with my mother when she had Anh and Thant. I had even helped my grandmother. I knew that Dao's cries sounded scary, but that most of the noise was just to help bring the baby into the world, like groaning and grunting when you carry a heavy pail of water up a hill. But Kim, who had never seen a baby being born, was frightened.

It seemed strange to me that Kim, whose mother was a doctor, knew so little about babies. "But she delivered babies in the hospital, not at home," Kim said. I thought that was a funny way to put it. If there was any "delivering," it was the mother who did it, not the doctor.

Kim's mother had offered her help to Dao, and Dao had looked hopefully at Tho for his permission to accept the *bac si*'s offer, but old Quang with great dignity had refused. Instead he invited our grandmother to attend Dao. The grandmother's harsh commands to Dao to "push" could be heard all over the boat. Tho was not allowed into the little enclosure with Dao and the grandmother. He sat miserably by himself, biting his lip and trying not to hear the jokes the men around him called out about the making of the baby.

Suddenly there was another cry, but it was not Dao. It was the strong squall of a baby, and the grandmother shouted, "A boy!" All over the boat people cheered. I remembered when Thant was born how pleased my father was to have a boy after having two girls. Even though I understood how important it was to have a son to carry on the family name and to venerate our ancestors, I was jealous of the attention Thant got. I had noticed that Kim's mother never seemed disappointed that Kim was not a boy.

I stole a look at Kim's mother to see if she was jealous because it was my grandmother and not her who helped Dao, but the *bac si* was grinning. "There is still hope," she said to my mother in a voice so soft I could barely hear the words.

The baby might have arrived on an auspicious day, but the day that followed brought bad luck. Early in the morning the boat sprung a leak and began to take on water. It was necessary to move some of the people in the hold to the deck, making things even more crowded than they had been before. We had to sit with our knees pressed against our chests and our arms clasped around our knees. A chain of men was organized to bail the boat out. Pails of water were passed up from the hold and dumped over the sides of the boat.

The "hold" people were happy to be on the deck, even in the hot sun. There were rats below, they said.

At night the rats came out and scrambled over you as you slept. Sometimes you could see their eyes glowing in the darkness like two points of fire. Lice had spread among the people in the hold and would now undoubtedly spread all over the boat.

But worse was to come. Around noon the engine stopped and the boat began to drift silently on the sea. The other times the motor had stopped my father had been able to get it started in a short while. There would be a few coughs and sputters and it would be working again. Captain Muoi would come out and reassure everyone that his boat was the best little boat in the world.

The engine failed at the hottest time of day. People sat as still as statues under any bits of shade they could find. The least movement brought you in contact with someone's hot sweaty body, and sometimes there were cross words. The new baby fretted and cried in the heat. Anh, who could not take her eyes off the baby, begged to be allowed to fan him gently with her straw hat. It was easier to put up with the heat and crowding when you knew the boat was going someplace. But the silence of the engine and the drift of the boat made you feel hopeless.

The sun slipped halfway down to the horizon before word was passed through the boat that a part in the engine had worn out and a new one was being made by my father from scraps of metal. No one knew whether the new part would work. As the news spread, there was a buzz of voices, but soon after that, silence, as though everyone were concentrating on my father being successful.

Kim and I were restless. I didn't think I could sit still for another minute. My mother spoke sharply to me. "When you squirm like that, Mai, you make it unpleasant for everyone around you."

"Let me get up for a little while," I pleaded. "Kim and I want to look out at the sea."

Each day we were allowed to pick our way over the tight rows of passengers to make our way to the boat railing. Once we had seen a school of porpoises rolling along one after the other in the wake of the boat. Another time we had been amazed to see sailfish leaping into the air and flying about. The strange flying fish made me think the whole world was upside down. More often there was nothing but the endless stretch of water.

"Go ahead, but try not to disturb too many people." I knew my mother's voice was impatient because she was afraid for my father. The lives of everyone in the boat depended on him.

No one in the boat was in a good mood, and there were many complaints as Kim and I made our way over the tangle of arms and legs to the boat railing. Each day, each hour, the color of the water changed. This afternoon it was a deep green. "Almost like grass," Kim said. I guessed she was thinking of how nice it would be to see land.

Suddenly Kim grabbed my arm and pointed. "Look!"

I looked in the direction Kim was pointing and saw a bit of timber floating on the water with something perched on top of it. Whatever it was moved. An animal? Something blowing in the late afternoon breeze? Then we heard a faint cry and saw the distant figure move as though an arm were waving to us.

"Someone is out there!" I shouted. The passengers scrambled to their feet and ran to the railing to see for themselves. The cabin door opened and we heard a roar. "What's going on? You fools! Get back where you belong. The whole boat is listing. We'll capsize!" It was Captain Muoi. He was right. I could feel the boat tilting as everyone hung over the side to get a better view.

They made way for the captain. "Quickly," someone called. "We're drifting away. We have to turn the boat around and pick him up."

"How can we turn the boat when there is no engine?" the captain shouted. He was pushing people back to their places. In the excitement Kim and I were overlooked. We hunched down out of sight and looked out over the railing at the distant figure floating in the sea.

"He will drown," I whispered to Kim. I couldn't take my eyes off the small shape bobbing in the water. Each time my eyes blinked the shape seemed to get smaller. Then the drift of the boat changed, and for a while we moved close enough to the wreckage so that we could hear the man's cries. Then the boat changed course again, and the wreckage with the clinging figure became a speck on the sea. Kim and I were holding each other's hands. I think it was because we couldn't reach out to the man that we held on to each other.

A small rasping noise came from the cabin and grew louder. The boat began vibrating, and in a minute it was plowing through the sea toward the distant speck. Captain Muoi grumbled good-naturedly about the extra fuel and the lost time the rescue would cost, but even he was excited. We were all quiet, thankful that it had not been our boat that had been wrecked. It might have been us out there alone on the sea.

"What could have caused the wreck?" Kim asked. "There haven't been any storms."

And why only one person? I wondered. Where were all the others?

As the boat drew close, we were shocked to see that it was a boy, not much older than Kim and I. The boy was staring at our boat at though it might be a vision that would suddenly disappear, leaving him all alone again.

My father cast a rope overboard, calling to the boy to tie it around his waist, but the boy was either afraid to let go of the bit of wreckage to which he was clinging or he did not understand what my father said, for he only continued to stare at us with blank eyes.

A second rope was tied around my father and he was lowered into the water. I closed my eyes. The sea was so large I didn't trust it. My father began to swim toward the boy. When my father reached the boy and began to circle his waist with a rope, the boy suddenly let go of the wreckage and threw his arms around my father, nearly strangling him. They both disappeared below the water. I heard my mother cry out.

A moment later they bobbed to the surface, a tangle of arms and rope. The boy was flailing out at my father, who was trying to get the rope around him. I clutched at Kim, nearly as scared as the boy. My father finally got an arm loose and slapped the boy's face so hard we heard the sound of it on the boat. The boy went limp and my father slipped the rope around him and began to swim back to the boat, an arm slung around the boy's body.

Hands reached over the side to haul at the ropes. The boy was hoisted into the boat, followed by my father, who climbed aboard panting and spitting water but proud of his catch. He laid the boy onto a mat.

Everyone pushed close to get a look at him. Kim's mother pleaded with them to keep back. The boy was shaking with fear. *Bac si* Hong ran practiced hands over the trembling boy and turned to the captain.

"There are no bones broken, but he's badly sun-burned and in shock. He's also suffering from dehydration."

Anh and Thant were sent to beg dry clothes for the boy. My mother handed him a cup from our ration of water. "Not too much at one time," Kim's mother cautioned.

Captain Muoi wanted to question the boy, but Kim's mother said "No!" in so strong a voice that the captain retreated without another word. At last the boy fell asleep, but it was a restless sleep. Several times during the night he woke the whole boat with screams that sounded as if ten thousand devils were after him. We didn't dare think about what nightmares he was having—or worse, that they might not be nightmares at all but memories.

8

I was awake early the next morning. The first thing I did was to look for the boy to be sure I hadn't dreamed his rescue. He lay curled up on a mat, his arms crossed over his chest, his legs bent at the knees and pressed against his body as though he were trying to curl up into the smallest shape possible so that nothing could get at him. His face was badly sunburned, but even so, I thought his high cheekbones and the curve of his mouth quite beautiful.

As I sat there staring at him, thinking it was surely a miracle that in all that sea our boat had found him, he opened his eyes and looked right at me. Quickly I looked away, embarrassed to have him catch me staring. But the boy did not seem to mind. He sat up. At first he appeared quite calm and looked around the boat as though he had been there for days and everything was familiar. The next moment a look came over his face of such terrible fear I could not bear to watch. He began to wail and scream, beating his hands and head against the deck.

Everyone was awake by then and scrambling to see what had happened. Captain Muoi ran from the cabin, stepping on a dozen people in his rush to get to the boy. Kim's mother had taken something out of her bag and I saw her jab a needle into the boy's arm. It wasn't long before his screaming stopped and the boy fell back onto the mat, silent and asleep.

Kim and I sat beside him all day, wanting him to awaken and tell us who he was but afraid that when he did awaken we would have to hear more of the terrible screams. We tried to guess what dreadful thing might have happened to him. The grandmother was sure the *ma da*, the ghosts of the water, had been after the boy and that even now they might have followed him and be all around us waiting to take us into the sea. At this, Anh began to cry and my mother had to beg the grandmother not to frighten her.

It was nearly evening when the boy awoke again. He was drowsy from the injection, but he no longer trembled and he seemed to know where he was. My mother offered him a little rice gruel, which he ate at once.

"Can you tell us your name?" Kim's mother asked gently.

"Vu Loi," the boy answered.

"What happened to you, Loi?" Kim's mother's voice was soft. "Should we look for other survivors?"

Everyone waited, hardly daring to breathe. Loi shook his head. "No. There are none." Tears fell from his eyes, but he seemed unaware of them, letting them fall on his chest and arms, making no effort to brush them away. "We were on a boat," he said in a lifeless voice, "not so large as this. My uncle's fishing boat. We were ten people, all escaping from the same village. For many months my uncle and father planned the trip. Every week for many weeks they put aside a little gasoline. They couldn't buy too much gasoline at one time or the government would be suspicious. They had to buy some on the black market and were afraid they would be found out. But finally we had enough.

"Some of us hid in the boxes where the fish were kept, and they put a piece of wood over us and ice on top as though they were going out for several days to fish. It was very cold, but we could not leave the chest until we were out at sea. Then we came on deck.

"When we were three days out we saw another boat. We thought they were people like us trying to escape. So we waved to them. When the boat came close, we saw that the men had long hair and axes and guns. We knew they were pirates. We tried to get away, but they rammed into our boat." Loi's hands began to tremble and his voice was only a whisper.

Kim's mother put a hand on his arm to let him know he did not have to continue, but now that he had begun it seemed he could not stop.

"They climbed into our boat and wanted gold, but we didn't have any. We were only fishermen. We tried to explain, but they were angry and began to chop holes in the boat. They took all our food and left us to drown. When the boat sank, we clung to what bits of wood we could find. We tried to stay together but . . ." He couldn't bring himself to say what had happened to everyone else. He hid his face in his arms.

As Loi told his story, the others had crept close to hear what he was saying. Now everyone was silent. We did not dare look into one another's faces. We had heard tales of the pirates who preyed on boats, but we had pretended not to believe them. We all slipped back to our places on the boat, trying to keep our eyes from the great empty stretch of water around us.

My grandmother rocked back and forth moaning softly to herself. "They will come and find us," she cried. "They are waiting out there for us. We are lost."

Kim thought the grandmother meant the pirates, but I knew she was speaking of the *ma da*, the ghosts of those who drowned on Loi's boat and who would not find peace until they had lured other victims to drown in the sea and take their place.

9

I was sure Loi would never want to look at the sea again, but it was not so. The next day he was feeling much stronger and he begged Kim's mother to let him move to a part of the deck where he could look out at the water. At first I thought he was hoping to see someone else from his boat, but it was really just the empty sea he was staring at.

Kim, who wasn't as shy with Loi as I was, asked him, "Doesn't the sea frighten you now?"

Loi said, "The sea is my home. I've lived all my life on a fishing boat. Someday I will have my own fishing boat. What happened was not the fault of the sea."

I never got tired of looking at Loi's face. Some faces are ugly when they are sad, but his was beautiful. I was careful, though, that he didn't catch me at it. I wished I could speak as easily with Loi as Kim could. But I didn't dare to. My grandmother muttered under her breath that a well-brought-up girl would never look a boy in the face and speak boldly with him as

Kim did. I thought that Kim was lucky and that her mother would probably let Kim marry anyone she pleased, while my parents would tell me whom I ought to marry. A hundred times I had heard my grandmother say, "Children must sit where their parents place them."

That afternoon everyone was still talking about Loi and what had happened to him when we were shocked to see my grandmother clutch her duck's neck and wring it. The squawks of the poor duck were terrible to hear. At first I thought all the food had run out. For several days the passengers had looked hungrily at the duck and begged my grandmother to kill it so they might all have a taste of meat or a bit of broth from the bones. They resented the rice it took to keep the duck alive, even though it came from my grandmother's small ration.

When I heard the duck's squawks I was frightened, but my mother had a smile on her face, the first one I had seen in a long time. "Don't you know what day it is?" she asked me.

Kim and I looked at each other, but we couldn't guess. It seemed like just another day of floating on the endless sea under a hot sun. My mother opened her basket. Anh and Thant pushed close. We had all wondered what she had in her basket. She reached inside and took out a small package, which she asked to have passed along to Captain Muoi.

At first Captain Muoi looked impatient, as though one more puzzle had been put into his hand. When he saw what it was, his frown disappeared. He reached into his pocket, and while everyone watched, he took out a packet of matches. A moment later there was an explosion overhead and the sky was filled with sparks. Firecrackers! Everyone on the boat began to call to one another in their excitement. We knew what the firecrackers meant. It was the first day of the lunar new year. The festival of Tet! That was why the duck had been killed. We would all have a taste of delicious meat—the first meat we had tasted since the trip began. My mouth watered hungrily as I thought of all the good food I had had on other Tet celebrations: pickled bean sprouts and sweet soybean soup and once a taste of bacon.

Everything in the boat changed. Neighbors who had been quarreling over a bit of space or a portion of rice made courteous apologies to one another. You never carried bad feelings into the new year. All debts and all arguments had to be settled. An angry word spoken on Tet would bring bad luck for the whole year.

Mother told us we had to clean ourselves up and wear the best clothes we had. The whole boat came alive. Le Hung plucked the duck. Feathers flew every which way over the railing and out onto the sea, where they rode the water like tiny boats. People called to one another with invitations to be the first visitor. The first visitor to your home on Tet must be someone who is well respected. My mother and grandmother were whispering together and I could tell they were trying to decide whom to ask. My grandmother was carefully avoiding looking at Kim's mother for fear she would be the one to give us our first Tet greeting. Finally they invited old Quang. He made a great ceremony of stepping the few inches from his own mat onto one of ours.

Not everyone felt about Kim's mother the way my grandmother did. One of the passengers whose son had been cured of a bad case of dysentery by *Bac si* Hong invited her to give them their first greeting. Our grandmother was scandalized that a woman would be chosen as the first visitor.

The captain with the help of my father was raising

a *cay neu*, a tall bamboo pole that was meant to look like a tree. If we had been back in our village a *cay neu* would have stood in front of every house. My grandmother gave a precious betel nut to go into a basket attached to the top of the pole as a gift to the god of the new year.

The duck was cooking on the stove, and the smell of the roasting bird was delicious. With the bamboo pole up and the duck roasting, it was time for the *giao thua*, the welcoming ceremony. The god of the old year was sent on his way and the god of the new year was welcomed.

Pleased to be the center of attention, my grandmother called out noisy instructions to Le Hung on how to divide the duck. Father and Thant were each to have an entire wing for themselves. A bit of skin and a morsel of meat were to go to me, to Anh and our mother, to Quang and his family, and to Captain Muoi and Loi. I knew my grandmother was in a good mood because she allowed Kim and even Kim's mother bits of skin and a morsel of meat—although they were to be smaller portions than ours. Le Hung was to have the same "and whatever he could lick from his fingers," the grandmother said.

Kim and I and Loi tried to guess what the grandmother would have for herself. "A whole leg," Kim guessed. "The neck," Loi said. I could see he was thinking of all the juicy shreds nestled between the neck bones. I guessed it would be the liver, crisp on the outside and pale pink and smooth on the inside.

But when we asked my grandmother, she shook her head and looked haughty. "It is my duck and I choose to give it all to the others. It will be added to the rice and everyone will have a taste." A murmur of awe went around the boat. Everyone was impressed. Our grandmother held her head high. The admiration of the other passengers tasted sweeter than the tender breast meat of the duck would have. After all the passengers had their rice and the lucky ones had found pieces of duck among the grains, the grandmother allowed Le Hung to coax her into accepting the drumstick of the duck to suck. "Only if you are sure all the meat is off of it," she said.

When Le Hung handed it to her I thought I saw a good-size chunk of meat on the bone, but my grandmother popped the drumstick into her mouth so quickly I could not be sure.

10

In the days that followed Tet we often thought about the taste of duck, for our food and water were running out and land was nowhere in sight. There was only one meal a day, and that was a small one. I tried not to think of my empty stomach. When night came I was too hungry to sleep. Without food and with only a few sips of water, Dao did not have enough milk to give her baby, and the baby cried and hiccuped most of the night.

The first thing everyone looked for on waking in the morning was a thin dark line on the horizon that would mean land. But the horizon was as empty as our rice bowls. One morning Loi went about the boat collecting bits and pieces of string. Kim and I watched him knot a fish net. His fingers moved quickly, forming loops. When he finished a set of loops, he ran string through each one of them. When he pulled all the strings tight—there was a square of mesh.

At last the net was ready to be lowered into the

water. I kept thinking of the big catfish we sometimes caught in the stream that ran through our village, but Loi said there were no catfish in the sea. Each time he drew up the net I was sure there would be something in it, but each time it was empty. "There is nothing for bait, and besides, the movement of the boat frightens the fish," Loi said. But we could not stop the boat. With our food and water nearly gone we had to find land in a hurry.

I was getting tired from standing in the glare of the hot sun and dizzy from not eating. The small ration of water everyone had been given that morning had left me thirstier than ever. I was looking at the cool green sea, wondering why there had to be so much water with salt in it, when I saw something floating on the surface of the sea. "Loi," I called. "Look. What is that?"

"A turtle!" He quickly drew up the net and threw it out just in front of the swimming turtle. The splash of the net frightened the turtle, and it veered away from the net, coming closer to the boat. I could see its brownish-green shell shaped like a great upside-down bowl. It had a thick head and hooded eyes. Its flippers worked slowly, pushing it along. Without taking the net out of the water, Loi slid it under the turtle and gave a quick jerk. The turtle rose out of the water with the net under it like a sling. Its head and feet disappeared into its shell. The flippers worked back and forth trying to swim out of the net into the air.

Loi swung the bamboo pole that held the net toward the boat, but just as the turtle was almost within reach, the tip of the pole, bent by the weight of the turtle, cracked, and the net and turtle fell into the water. In a second Loi was over the side of the boat and holding on to the turtle. I screamed for help. Someone threw a rope, but instead of tying it around himself, Loi wrestled it around the struggling turtle. "Pull!" he shouted.

Hands reached for the turtle, and the rope was cast out again to Loi, who used it to pull himself up to the boat's edge where the men could boost him onto the deck.

The turtle was at least three feet across and ugly. As hungry as I was, I didn't think I could eat anything that looked like that. "They're delicious," Kim told me. "We used to make soup from them."

I decided cities might not be such special places if that was what people ate. I couldn't watch the men pry the turtle's shell apart to get at the meat. I kept thinking of how much I had felt like a turtle without its shell when I was leaving our house. That made me sorry for the turtle, but when the time came to eat it, I was so hungry I took a small piece. It tasted like chicken, and I ate it greedily.

"I told you so," Kim said.

But the little bit of food only sharpened everyone's appetite. The insides of the turtle had been carefully saved for bait. Loi and some of the men made fishing lines and threw them overboard. They thought they were sure to catch something until they saw a sharp black fin skim the surface of the water. "Shark," Loi said. "He's after the bait and the hooks are too small to hold him." A moment later the bait was gone.

As the afternoon grew hotter, *Bac si* Hong warned Kim and me not to move around so much. "Stay on your mats," she said. "Movement makes you warm and that makes you perspire. It's important that you should not lose any water from your body when there is so little water to replace it." But sitting with nothing to do made you think about how thirsty you were.

There was talk over how the small amount of water we had left ought to be divided. Some thought it ought to go to the old people, who seemed to feel the heat the most. Others said it should go to the children. "To the boys," our grandmother said. "They will carry on the family name."

Kim was shocked at this and started to answer my grandmother back, but her mother hushed her. "It is not a time for quarreling," she said.

For once our grandmother and Kim's mother were working together. Quang had fallen sick. He could not speak and part of his body was paralyzed. His right leg would not support him, and his right arm lay useless at his side. There had been a question of who would attend him. Dao and her husband wanted Kim's mother, but everyone knew that if the old man could speak he would have asked for the grandmother.

The grandmother was too proud to push herself forward, but she watched with a skeptical eye as Kim's mother examined Quang. When the examination was

over, Kim's mother bowed gracefully to our grandmother and indicated that she would be glad to have
the grandmother do her own examination. Pretending
to be indifferent, the grandmother bent over the old
man. He lay with his eyes closed, his chest heaving.
I found myself holding my breath, waiting for Quang's
next breath to come. When my grandmother was finished she and Kim's mother looked at each other. My
grandmother shook her head sadly. Kim's mother
nodded agreement.

"There is nothing to be done," the grandmother
told Tho and Dao, "beyond prayer and incantations
to insure the easy passage of his soul."

They turned to Kim's mother. She agreed. "Beyond prayers, there is nothing that can be done."

Tho and Dao looked frightened. "If he should die
at sea there would be no proper coffin and no burial
ground," Tho said. He pleaded with the grandmother
and the *bac si*. The grandmother rubbed Quang's useless arm and leg with some salve and repeated a number of incantations, explaining that if any of Quang's
three souls and nine vital spirits had departed from
his body—as certainly they had—he could not live.

Her incantations would beg the souls and spirits to return, but she was sure it was too late.

Kim's mother gave Quang some pills, which he was able to swallow only with great difficulty, but neither the pills nor the incantations helped. Quang slipped into a deeper sleep. He lay still as a statue. His breathing became so light you could not see his chest move unless you looked closely. In the evening he died. A great silence came over the boat, broken only by the sobbing and wailing of Tho and Dao.

At first I was afraid to look at Quang. I had never been that near to a dead person. But he lay so close to us it was impossible not to see him. I was relieved to find that he appeared quite peaceful. Dao and my grandmother had carefully dressed him and wrapped his head in a turban. His thin face with the high cheekbones and the scraggly beard and the long thin body looked like the statues that lay upon the tombs of ancient emperors. I had seen pictures of such tombs in my history book.

One by one the passengers came to offer their sympathy. Le Hung spared us a few grains of rice to put into Quang's mouth so that he would not be hungry on the journey to his next life. But there was not enough rice or tea for the ritual offerings. Finally the captain came and with many apologies explained that it was time for the burial. With great dignity the body was wrapped in a tarpaulin and, with Dao and Tho leading the way, was carried the few feet to the boat's edge and gently lowered into the sea. Tho recited five prayers that entreated the soul of his father to leave his grave in the sea and return to the altar of their ancestors.

I thought this was the saddest part of all, for until Dao and Tho found a home, there would be no altar for Quang to return to, only the sea.

After the burial, no one said much. I could see that many of the passengers were thinking of other burials. Everyone on the boat had lost relatives in the many years of the war and the new government. Kim would be thinking of her father. Loi? Who knew what sad thoughts must be going through Loi's head? I could not even look at him. Then something more terrible occurred to me. Suppose we never found land? Our food and water were nearly gone. Would we all be slipped, one by one, into the shark-filled sea like old Quang?

Others must have been thinking the same thing, for an argument was going on in the cabin over the direction the boat was taking. Loi wanted the captain to change the course of the boat. Loi insisted he was right because of the position of the stars and where the moon rose at night and the sun set and the way the winds blew. Most of the men believed Loi, for the journey was taking nearly three weeks, but Captain Muoi resented Loi's interference. If the boy was right he, Captain Muoi, must be wrong. At last he agreed to try Loi's course "for one night only."

I watched the moon rise. As it climbed, it left a trail of silver footprints on the water. Loi explained to Kim and me that each night the moon rose in a slightly different place and that you could predict where those places were. That seemed strange to me. In all the space of the sky, how did the moon know where it should be? What kept it from being like our boat, just drifting on the sea of sky?

As I lay down to sleep, I noticed that there was a bit more space than usual. I didn't have to curl my legs up quite as much. Grateful for the new comfort, I stretched out. Then I realized that the reason there was more room was because Quang had died. It was his empty space. Feeling guilty, I pulled up my legs. Suppose his spirit was still with us, floating aimlessly about until Tho and Dao found a home where they could prepare a proper altar for Quang and the rest of their ancestors?

All night I lay in my cramped position, leaving Quang's small space open.

PART FOUR

The Silver City

11

"Mai! Wake up!"

I opened my eyes. My arms and legs were so cramped I could hardly move. My empty stomach ached. Even in the cool morning my throat was dry. I saw people crowding toward the railing.

Kim was shaking me. "Mai! You can see buildings!"

I sat up. Anh, who was curled up next to me, awakened and looked around as if the buildings might be right in the boat. Our mother hurried after Thant, who was hanging over the railing. Anh and I followed Kim. The passengers were cheering. A few were silent, just looking and looking as though they could not get enough of what they saw. Kim pointed to the horizon, where I saw the silver city just as it was on Diep Van Tien's postcard. I had never quite believed there could be such a place, but there it was. Hundreds of buildings rose out of the sea and stretched unbelievably high into the air. "How do people get to the top?" I asked Kim.

She gave me a surprised look. "Why, they have elevators," she said. But that meant nothing to me.

Kim's mother put an arm around Kim. Our father sat Thant on his shoulders so that Thant could see better. Dao was bouncing the baby and chattering excitedly to Tho. My grandmother was on her knees offering thanks to the spirits that had kept us from drowning. I couldn't stop staring at the buildings. They looked as if they had been created at that very moment out of thin air.

Captain Muoi was taking all the credit for getting us to Hong Kong, but I saw my father wink at Loi. There was so much commotion, no one spoke of our hunger pains or how thirsty we were. It had been two days since we had eaten, but my father said there would soon be food for everyone. When I looked at all the buildings towering into the sky, I was not sure. Where were all the farms that grew the food?

As we drew closer to shore, we saw boats of all sorts and sizes, some as big as our whole village. There were sampans and junks and lots of beautiful white boats ten times larger than our boat. "They are yachts," Kim's mother said, "and they belong to just one person." One person for all that boat, and we had forty people crowded onto ours!

The sampans and junks were all around us, hundreds and hundreds of them. "Look," Anh said, "they have little houses on the boats."

"And chickens," said Thant hungrily.

It was true. There were gardens growing on the decks and dogs and chickens and children running around. The water was almost covered with boats. We heard music, and there was the delicious odor of food being cooked. Some of the people on the boats waved to us, calling friendly words, but others waved their fists and shouted, "Go back where you came from. You are not wanted here." Some of those who shouted angry words shouted in our own language.

We drew back from the railing of the boat, for the angry words were flung at us like stones and hurt us after our long, hard trip. I saw the *bac si* tighten her lips, as I had seen her do before when she was angry. She said, "Some of those people came here just as we did, and now that they are safe they don't want others to come."

"Will we have to go back?" Dao asked Tho in a shaky voice.

"Never," he said. "I will never go back."

We steered our way through the crowded maze of boats. The closer we came to the shore the taller the buildings grew, until I had to bend my head back to find the tops. Now we could see cars and people on the shore, more cars and people than I could have imagined.

Kim was not looking at the shore but at a barge that was approaching us. On it were men in uniform. "Policemen," Kim said in a frightened voice. I tried to convince her not to worry. "Policemen here," I said, "will not be like the policemen in Vietnam."

The barge signaled to us to throw them a line and they would tow us to shore. "It is only that they want to help us," my father said, but his voice was unsure.

I thought there would be the same rush to get off the boat as there was to get on. Instead, after saying goodbye to Captain Muoi, who appeared sad to see us leave, we all climbed onto the wharf in an orderly fashion. "I told you I would get you here safely," the captain called after us.

A woman from our own country welcomed us. "I am Binh," she said, "and I am here to help you." But behind the polite woman were several officers who indicated that we were to get onto a bus that waited for us. I saw one of the passengers try to slip into the crowds on the wharves, but two officers quickly brought him back.

"They have a bus to meet us," our mother said, trying to make it sound as though it were a courtesy.

The grandmother whimpered. "They are not meeting us," she said. "They are taking us prisoner."

"Hush," our father said. "You don't know what you are saying. There are authorities here as everywhere. Would you have a country with no rules? We must hear their rules and then they will let us go."

Kim's mother shook her head. "I am afraid one of the rules will be that they will not let us go."

At first I thought my father was right, for the officers and the woman were very kind to us, smiling and helping the older ones and the children onto the bus. But when the bus door snapped shut, I felt for a moment as though I were one of the little mice my mother trapped to keep them from eating our rice.

As the bus traveled through the city, I forgot my worries, for there was so much to see that I had never seen before. I sat next to Kim and could not help grabbing her arm. "Look at all the food!" On both sides of the streets were shops. A row of ducks dangled inside one shop. Crates of live chickens and geese were stacked in another. There were neat piles of strange fruits and pyramids of bright-colored vegetables—red tomatoes, purple eggplants, green and yellow peppers. There were cucumbers that looked nearly as tall as Thant. A sigh went through the bus of hungry passengers. "There's enough for everyone," I said.

"You have to have money to buy those things," Kim told me.

After the food streets there were streets of furniture and streets of clothes. There was one shop full of only blue jeans. Kim smiled at me. After a while the bus left the streets of shops and passed through streets of large square brick buildings with no windows. Men were carrying heavy boxes from the buildings and loading them onto huge trucks. "Those buildings are warehouses," Kim said.

"What are warehouses?" I asked.

"They are big buildings where people store things until they are needed," Kim told me.

Our bus pulled up to one of the warehouses. "Perhaps they are going to get some things for us," I said. Instead we were told to get off the bus. Binh led us through a door into the warehouse. We were taken to a room where we were given water and rice while we waited. Then one by one we went in to see a woman. Kim's mother said the woman was a nurse.

"They want to be sure we have no diseases that we might give to the other refugees," she said. When the nurse heard that Kim's mother was a doctor, she hurried out to greet her.

"I only wish that you could help us," the nurse said. "We have hundreds who are sick and not enough doctors to take care of them."

"Of course I will help," the *bac si* said.

"You don't understand," the nurse told her. "Vietnamese doctors are not allowed to help. It is forbidden in Hong Kong." The *bac si* said nothing, but I saw her tighten her lips. There was a look in her eyes that made me think she would do as she pleased.

When we had all been fed and examined, a man

talked to each family to ask why we had come to Hong Kong. At last we were led through a large door into a room. I couldn't believe my eyes. The room was as large as a rice field, and it was full of people. Hundreds and hundreds of people. Small platforms were lined up row after row and even stacked one above the other into triple decks. The platforms were only as wide as I was tall and about twice as long. On each of the platforms was a family. Frightened, I turned to Kim. "You didn't say they kept people in the warehouses." But Kim had left me and was holding on to her mother.

Pham Van Tho was speaking angrily to Binh. "You cannot put us here. This is not why we came to Hong Kong. Let us go. We want to work and earn our living. If you don't want us in your city, then send us to another country."

Binh shook her head and looked as though she did not want to say what she was going to say. "There are thousands like you who have come here from Vietnam," she told Tho. "We have no place for you. There are no houses and no jobs, and other countries can take only a few of you. This is the best we can do. You will be fed here, and we will see what we can do to help you, but it will take time." The worst thing about what she said was that she sounded as though she had said it to many people many times before.

We wanted to stay with our friends from the boat, but we had to go where there were empty platforms. We were directed to a top one. We climbed a small ladder. The grandmother had to be helped up it. Thant climbed up like a little monkey. He thought it was fun to live on what he called "the roof." When our family was together, our mother said in a frightened whisper, "We have no privacy here." And it was true. The first and second layers of platforms had roofs and little curtains, but the top decks had no place for curtains.

"But we have the light," my father said. The lower platforms were darker because of their roofs and curtains. The man on the top platform next to us called a welcome. "I am Nguyen," he said, "and this is my wife, Ly. Where do you come from?" We exchanged the names of our villages, but theirs was in the north and ours in the south. Still, they were very friendly and eager to hear about our voyage and even more eager to tell us about theirs. They had come to Hong Kong because Ly's father had been arrested by the government. They had worried that they, too, might be arrested.

"The food is not bad," Nguyen said. "Certainly it is better than in Vietnam. And here there is always the chance that another country may take you in."

"What about the family who had this platform before we came?" Father asked.

Nguyen was about to answer when his wife nudged him and shook her head. He was quiet for a moment and then he said, "No, it is better that they know everything so they will be prepared. The family that had your platform has been sent back to Vietnam. Several families were put on a plane and flown back."

Thant, who had been listening with wide eyes and an open mouth, now said, "I want to go back so I can ride on a plane."

Father was angry with Thant. "You don't know what you are saying. Just think what we have gone through to come here so that we may keep from starving and so that your grandmother and I are not put in prison. You are a stupid boy to think of giving up freedom for a ride on a plane." He turned to Nguyen. "Can they make you go back?"

"For some families it is difficult to stay here. After you live like this for many weeks and with no chance of going to another country you become discouraged. Also, they give you money to go back. This family received one hundred twenty-eight dollars in American money."

At this the grandmother sighed. "That is more money than I have seen in my whole life," she said. "For that I might go back."

"I am surrounded by fools," Father said. After that he sat without saying a word, his head bowed. The grandmother was silenced by his sad look. Thant crept close to Father and looked up at him with tears in his eyes. He knew he had said something to make Father angry, but he didn't know exactly what. Father took a deep breath and said, "We must be thankful that we have arrived safely. Now let's go and find the others."

Mother and the grandmother stayed to unpack our mats and our few clothes. Thant and Anh also stayed. I think they were afraid of going among so many people. But I was eager to see Kim—and Loi. We found Tho and Dao and their baby only a few rows from us. Dao was unhappy. "It is so noisy in here, worse than on the boat. The baby frets and won't sleep, and the people underneath us are complaining because of his crying." She tried to appear more cheerful. "At least I have food to give the baby."

Tho added, "The people beneath us have been here for many weeks. They are elderly and have little chance of going to another country, and they are not wanted here in Hong Kong. They complain about the baby because they are unhappy and who can blame them?"

Loi came running up. "I am over there," he said, pointing to a platform a few rows away. There were three boys on the platform. One of them was Loi's age, the others a little older. "They are my new friends," he said. "One of them is a fisherman like me, and the other two come from Ho Chi Minh City. They know how to get extra food, and each boy has two pairs of blue jeans for himself. They said if I stay with them and do what they say, they will get me some, too."

My father shook his head. "Loi, you are in a country now where you must think for yourself. What do you know of these boys?"

Loi shrugged. He didn't like my father scolding him. "Why shouldn't I have friends?" he asked.

Perhaps thinking of all Loi had gone through and how he had lost his family, my father said, "I'm glad you have found friends. Only remember a friend must be someone you can trust."

Loi walked slowly back to his row and climbed up to his platform. The other boys looked our way and laughed. They said something to Loi that Loi must not have liked, for he turned away from them, but after a minute he forgot us and joined the other boys in their laughter.

12

It took us a while to find Kim and her mother. *Bac si* Hong was happy to see us. "I've been looking everywhere for you. There are so many sick people here. They tell me I cannot help, but I will not see people sick and do nothing. I will do what I must, but I must do it secretly. I am afraid to leave Kim alone. Not everyone in the camp can be trusted. Could Kim stay with you for a little while?"

"We would be honored," my father said. I was surprised to hear him add, "*Bac si* Hong, you have more knowledge about these things. What will happen to us here?"

In front of my mother, Father had been sure of himself, but now he was turning to Kim's mother for help. I saw that he was more worried than he had shown. And more surprising than anything, he was asking help from a woman.

Kim's mother shook her head. "I knew we would have to stay in a camp of some kind, but I had no idea it would be like this. We are no better than chickens in a coop. I have learned that those who have relatives in another country or who speak the language of another country or even have a skill that would be wanted have the best chance of finding a home there."

"Then you and Kim are lucky," Father said. "You speak English, and a doctor is surely wanted."

"Maybe," she said, "but for the moment there is much for me to do here. Only it bothers me that I must do it secretly. You have relatives in America who will help." We had shown our uncle Tien's postcard to *Bac si* Hong on the boat.

For a moment my father smiled, but the smile quickly disappeared. "America must be large. How would we ever find Tien?"

"You must ask Binh," Kim's mother said. "I think she wants to help us. You must also tell them you are a skilled mechanic."

Kim and I begged to explore the large room, but my father hurried us back to our platform. "Have you lost your modesty? Would you wander among all these strangers? Listen to those terrible sounds." There was a radio playing loud music such as I had never heard.

"We had that music in Ho Chi Minh City," Kim said. "It is called rock."

"A good name for it," Father said. "It is hard music and loud enough to crack your head."

When we returned to our little space, we found that our mother had learned a great deal from our neighbor Ly. Mother was proud of her new knowledge and seemed less worried. "I know of a place where I can wash our clothes. Although there is only cold water. Also, the family below us has children the same ages as Thant and Anh. Thant and Anh are with them now. The family hopes to be leaving in a week or two. They have promised us their place and we shall have curtains and a roof over our heads." Mother said all this in a rush of words.

I could see the words pleased my father, but the grandmother only said, "This is what you have brought me to. I told you we should never have come." Then she saw that Kim had her flute with her and the grandmother smiled. "Come and sit beside me and play your music for me. The sounds are strange, but if I close my eyes I can see our village."

As Kim played on her flute everyone was not quiet,

as they had been on the boat when she played. In the big room radios played loudly and people shouted to one another. Babies cried and there were loud coughs. Still, in all that noise a little island of silence grew around us. Even Loi's friends were quiet, staring hard at Kim's flute.

As the time for supper drew near, people began to call out impatiently for their food. At last the doors into the room opened and several carts appeared loaded with great buckets of steaming rice and smaller pails of vegetables. There were complaints from many of the families of small portions. We did not complain, for we had not had vegetables for many days. As one of the carts was rolling down our aisle, we heard a cheerful voice call to us. Dishing out the food was Le Hung. "When they found out I was a cook they brought me to the kitchen," he said. "What better job than to be with food all day? Here, pass me your bowls." Hung gave each of us a generous serving of the vegetables. With a quick look over his shoulder to see if anyone was watching, Hung handed a folded lettuce leaf to the grandmother. "You were generous with your duck," he said, and grinned. Tucked inside the leaf were several large shrimp. The grandmother nodded to Hung, and after he had rolled his cart away she handed out one shrimp to each of us, not forgetting Kim and giving Thant two large ones.

We had just finished our supper when Kim's mother came for her. "There is so much to do," she said in a tired voice. "There are children with measles, which could spread through the whole camp. What is worse, no one seems to keep track of who has been vaccinated. I have no medicines to give. And I must do everything in secret."

She smiled at the grandmother. "You are needed too," she told her. "A woman who is having nightmares and cannot sleep has asked for someone who can chase away the evil spirits. I said I knew just such a person."

The grandmother looked pleased and said, "It is something I have done a hundred times."

"Also, she has a little money and will reward whoever can help her. Tomorrow I will take you to her." The grandmother looked doubly pleased.

As it grew later, we waited for the lights to be turned off so that we could sleep. They were dimmed a little, but it was hard to close our eyes. On the top platform we were directly under the lights. "Nguyen," Father called to our neighbor, "when will they turn off the lights?"

"Oh, the lights are never turned off. There are thieves here. If they turned off the lights, no one would dare to sleep."

13

We could not believe that anyone would steal from people who had so little, but the next morning, when Kim's mother brought Kim to us for the day, we saw that Kim had been crying. *Bac si* Hong was very angry. "Last night while Kim and I were asleep someone came and took Kim's flute. How could they be so cruel? They will sell it for much less than it is worth, and there is no way I can replace it."

"But with the lights," my father said, "surely someone must have seen who took it."

"Those around us were asleep, too. Even if they weren't, it is very dangerous to report a thief here. The thief would find a way to avenge himself against anyone who informed on him."

We all tried to cheer Kim up, but it is hard to cheer up someone else when you are none too happy yourself. When my father was called in to see Binh he was told many people would be sent back to Vietnam, and she urged him to agree to join them. When he refused and begged to be sent to another country, Binh said the only thing in his favor was his skill as a mechanic.

Father said, "Binh asked if I knew anyone in another country, and I showed her the postcard from Tien. The government here lists people by their villages as well as by their name. Also, they keep track of where they go. It is very remarkable. Binh said she might be able to find Tien and his family. It is nothing we can count on. Still it is a hope."

Hope was all we had during those days that became weeks. One of the worst things was that there was little water to bathe in and no soap. We began to itch all over, and Kim's mother said we had scabies. Scratching was just about all we had to do. Each day was like the day before. At first we went about and visited with the people from our boat, but after a while we grew discouraged and just stayed on our platform. Loi did not come to see us, and the one time that Kim and I went to visit him he seemed uncomfortable with us. We thought he cared only for his new friends. When Loi was not with his friends he was standing in line by the window. There was only one window in our warehouse room. It was high up. If you wanted a chance to see the sun and the sky you had to wait for a turn to step on the wooden box beneath the window. For just a quick glimpse of the sky you had to wait for an hour or more, but Loi was often in the line.

We had been in Hong Kong nearly four weeks when Loi climbed up to see us in the middle of the night. In his hand was Kim's flute. "Quickly, take this and hide it until I am gone," he whispered. His hand was trembling.

"Where are you going?" I asked.

"I am going back to Vietnam," he said. "We leave for another camp in a few minutes."

Once before the officials had come in the middle of the night to round up people to send back to Vietnam. Some of the people had agreed to return; others did not want to go back. Everyone in the camp was afraid they might be made to return. Some people who thought they were on the list to go back would change beds with other refugees so that the officials could not find them. "Loi, why do you want to go back to Vietnam?" Father asked.

"There is no hope for me here. What country wants a boy who has no skill but fishing? And I miss the sea. I could not stand being shut up here any longer."

He looked warily over his shoulder. "Also, it is dangerous for me. I want to get away from them." He pointed to the sleeping boys on his platform. "You were right to warn me," he said to my father. "Those boys stole Kim's flute. I tried to make them give it back, but they threatened me. I didn't dare tell you or they would have beaten me—or worse. I had to wait until I knew I was leaving to return the flute."

"I wish you wouldn't go," Anh said. Like Anh, I also wished Loi would not go, but I could not bring myself to say it. I was only brave enough to squeeze Loi's arm.

Loi smiled at me and seemed to cheer up. "They are giving all of us who go back some money. With that I can buy an interest in a fishing boat. And I will get to ride in a plane." He patted Anh and Thant on the head. As he climbed down from our platform, the doors opened and the officials came in to round up the refugees. Loi hurried over to them, glad of their protection, but many families complained bitterly at being sent back and vowed that however long it took they would return to Hong Kong. Some families cried and begged to stay. I put my hands over my ears to keep from hearing the terrible sounds.

"One day it will be our turn," the grandmother said.

The rest of the night I stayed awake, unable to sleep. I remembered the sad cries of those who were being sent away. I knew that we would probably never see Loi again. The only thing that cheered me was the thought of how happy Kim would be when she saw her flute.

14

The next morning, Kim could hardly believe her eyes. She had to hear the story of Loi appearing in the middle of the night twice. Kim's mother said, "It was very brave of Loi to return the flute." Something in *Bac si* Hong's voice made us stop talking about the flute and ask her what was wrong. "I will tell you because Kim will have to stay with you, but you must not tell the others." She lowered her voice. "There is cholera in the camp."

Mother put her hand across her mouth to keep from crying out. The grandmother shook her head. "There is nothing to be done for that." There had been cholera epidemics in our village. "For all my herbs and potions I have never found a way to cure those who fall sick with cholera." It was not often the grandmother admitted that there was something she could not cure.

"Fortunately," the *bac si* said, "in Hong Kong they have medicines and vaccines that will cure the sick, but it will take time to vaccinate everyone. Also, it is important that the water and food are not contaminated. Meanwhile there may be many who will be sick, and there are few to care for them. Still they will not let me help. Everything I do must be done when those in charge of the camp are not watching."

In only a day's time several people fell ill. Dao was so weak she could do nothing for her baby. Tho had all he could do to watch over Dao. Mother offered to care for the baby and Kim and I helped. Our neighbor Nguyen was so ill we could hear his groans all night. We hardly saw the *bac si*. When she came to see Kim, her hair, usually so neatly pulled back from her face, was untidy, and there were circles under her eyes. "I have had very little sleep," she said. "But that is nothing. What worries me is that an officer in the camp has caught me helping the sick. He is threatening to send me back to Vietnam, but as long as I am needed I won't stop."

By the end of the week she told us, "I think the epidemic is under control. Almost everyone has been vaccinated." "Almost," because there were a few people who hid from the nurses and would not be stuck with a needle. The grandmother was one of them. Nothing my father could say would convince her that the vaccination was necessary. "No one will squeeze poison into me," she insisted.

It must have been because she was so stubborn that the grandmother would not tell us she was feeling sick. She was also a little ashamed of refusing the vaccination. We noticed that when Le Hung came with the special bits of food he saved for her, she would not eat. Soon she was so ill we didn't know what to do. Her eyes bulged out under her closed lids and she moaned that she was going to die.

Father went for Kim's mother. After she examined the grandmother, the *bac si* said, "She will have to be moved to the hospital at once. She is very sick." But the grandmother was not so sick that she did not angrily refuse to go to the hospital. "I will die if they take me away."

The *bac si* gave in. "It is true," she said to us, whispering so that my grandmother could not hear. "It would be hard for her. They do not speak Vietnamese at the hospital, and they would not understand her. I have made friends with the nurse, and it may be that she will give me some medicine."

Like my grandmother, many people would not admit how sick they were. They were afraid of being taken away from their families. No one was allowed to visit the hospital. The doctors and nurses did not speak our language. Worst of all was the worry that while they were gone their families would be sent back to Vietnam. Because they would not go to the hospital, many did not get well. There would be cries of sorrow in the night, and you knew that someone had died from cholera.

The grandmother was lucky. In a few days she was better and looking for Le Hung to see what good thing he might bring her to eat. Dao was better too, and had her baby back.

It was two weeks before the *bac si* was finally able to take Kim back. "I'm going to sleep around the clock," the *bac si* said.

That night the officers again came to return people to Vietnam. Our neighbors Nguyen and Ly were taken. Ly was weeping as they left. "How can we believe it will be safe to return," she asked, "when my father is still in prison? And we will be hungry again." But their pleading to stay made no difference, and they were taken away.

For a long time after that none of us could sleep. When we finally did it seemed only moments before

I felt a tug on my arm. I woke with a start. Kim had climbed our ladder and was sitting on our platform. She was trying not to make any noise, but I could see her shoulders shaking with sobs. I woke my mother and father. My mother put her arms around Kim. "What is it?" she whispered.

"They have taken my mother back to Vietnam." She was crying so hard that we could hardly make out the words.

"Why?" I asked, scarcely able to believe what she was telling us.

"Last night the father of the family next to us had pains in his belly. They asked my mother for help, so she examined the man and said that his appendix must come out right away. She told the family to ask that the man go at once to the hospital. The officer said it was night and the man must wait until the next morning. My mother was very angry and she went to the officer and said the man might die if he didn't get to the hospital. The officer asked her how she knew that. She said she was a doctor and she had examined the man. The officer said that was against the rules. He would not take the man.

"This morning the man was very sick, and my

mother went to the head of the camp. She told him about the officer who was on duty last night and how he would not send the man to the hospital. Then they sent the sick man to the hospital right away and they scolded the officer. The officer was very angry with Mother. Tonight when they came to take the others to be sent to Vietnam, the officer said Mother must go too." Kim put her hands over her face.

"They didn't try to take you?" my father asked.

Kim shook her head. "Mother saw them coming and she told me to hide in the platform of the people below us. They have been our friends. When the officers were gone, I was to come to you. Mother said they were just angry with her and would not look for me. At first I wouldn't go, but she cried and begged me so hard I finally did what she told me to. She said she did not care for herself, but that I must have a chance to go to school and to study music. She believes that you will be lucky and go to America. But I wish I had gone with my mother. I would rather be in Vietnam if I could be with her."

It was many hours before Kim stopped crying and many days before she would eat more than a small bite of food. Some days she did not talk at all.

Kim's sadness was catching. We began to lose hope for ourselves and worried that like Kim's mother, we too would be sent back to Vietnam. My mother's eyes often had tears, and my father became more silent each day. There was nothing to do but sit in our little space. After a while we didn't even want to be awake. We went to bed earlier and earlier and got up later and later. The more we slept the quicker the time went by. Kim would not play her flute, even for our grandmother.

Thant and Anh whined and quarreled when they were awake. They had nothing to do and no one to play with. The family with the two children on the platform beneath us had gone to England. Just as they promised, they had given us their platform, and now we had a roof and a curtain to draw around us. Longer and longer each day the curtain stayed closed while we slept, trying to get through the long hours of waiting.

On one of those mornings when we were sleeping, Binh pulled the curtain open hastily. "Wake up!" she cried. "I have news for you. We have found Diep Van Tien and his family in America, and they have agreed to sponsor you."

"What must we do?" Our father's voice was eager. Even the grandmother was sitting up, looking interested.

"Go to the English classes. Prepare yourselves."

We had known about the classes, but we had not attended them because my father said we should not show that we believed we were going to America. If we were too confident, the spirits might punish us. They would think it arrogant to take such a thing for granted. Kim would not go to the classes. "I already know English," she said. "Anyhow, I don't care now." Thant and Anh and I went to the children's school, and our father went to a class with other men. I did not expect the grandmother to come with us, but I coaxed our mother. "Why don't you come? There are classes for the women."

"No," our mother said. "I am too old."

"There are many women older than you are," I told her. But she would not go to the class. She was too shy, afraid that a woman from a small village would appear foolish in the eyes of the other women. Each afternoon when I came back from class I would show her my workbook and teach her some of the things I had learned. In that way she picked up many words. She laughed at herself, but she was proud of her new skill.

She said, "I must learn so that I can understand when all you children begin to talk together, or in no time you will plot behind my back." It was true that we often spoke English to one another, for Anh and Thant thought the sounds of the English words very funny.

The days began to go by more quickly. Finally the day came when Binh led us into the office to talk with the woman who was in charge of where everyone went. We could hardly believe that the Americans would take us, that the time would come for us to leave the camp and Hong Kong. We thought if we were lucky enough to be able to go, we would have several days, perhaps weeks to get ready. Instead, a flight was leaving the next day. We were to be on it.

My mother flew to the laundry to scrub and iron all of our clothes. My father took his tools out and carefully cleaned and polished them. Thant and Anh and I practiced our English words. Only Kim and the grandmother were quiet. "Now we are a long way from our village and our ancestors," the grandmother said. "Soon we will be many thousands of miles farther. How can I rejoice?" Kim said nothing, but I knew she was thinking of how far from her mother she would be in America.

We were ready in our clean clothes long before it was time to leave. We had thought we would have no sadness at leaving Hong Kong. But it was not so. On hearing our good news, our friends from the boat came to say good-bye. Dao and Tho begged us to remember them. Tho was discouraged. No one seemed to want them, and soon all the baby would know of life was the long days spent on his tiny platform in the crowded room. "We wish you well," Tho said. "We are happy for you, but don't forget us here. Perhaps you will find a way to bring us to you."

"We'll do everything we can," our father promised.

There were a dozen of us from our camp going to America. Refugees from the other camps in Hong Kong would join us. But even so, we were only a very few. Thousands and thousands would remain behind. It was hard to be happy.

Anh and Thant could only think of riding on an airplane. Sometimes when we were working in the rice fields we would look up at the sky and watch the planes fly over us like strange birds. We never thought we would be in one.

As we stopped at one camp after another to pick up passengers, the bus became crowded. The grandmother had been so troubled by the thought of the long trip, she had eaten almost nothing. Now, sickened by the lurching bus, she became weak and dizzy. Binh saw her trouble and told us not to worry. "I understand that one of the refugees who will be going is a doctor."

At the next camp people crowded into the bus. Suddenly Kim, who was sitting next to me, jumped from her seat. She fought her way through the aisle toward the door. I ran after her, afraid she was trying to escape the bus that would take her farther away from her mother. In a minute I saw who she was running toward. It was her mother. The *bac si* pushed people aside to get her arms around Kim. She hugged me too, and then she threw her arms around my mother and father and kissed Anh and Thant. She even kissed the grandmother, who looked shocked but who seemed to be over her dizziness.

Our father could hardly speak. "We thought you

were back in Vietnam. How did you get here? How did you know we were leaving?"

"When I got to the detention camp where I was to stay until they sent me back to Vietnam, I pretended I was very sick. Since I am a doctor, it was easy to imitate a sickness. I knew all the symptoms. They took me to the hospital. At the hospital I told my story to the doctors there. I told them how I had tried to help a man who was very ill. How I was punished for that by the guard at our camp. How it was the guard who made them take me away in the middle of the night. How I had to leave Kim so she would not have to go back to Vietnam.

"The doctors were very angry. One of the doctors was a volunteer from a hospital in America. He wrote to his hospital and asked them to sponsor me so that I could come to America. I could not go back to your camp because of the official, who would have reported me, but through the doctors I was able to learn that you were going to America and when you would leave. And here I am!"

The bus was lumbering to a place where there were many large buildings. There were huge fields, and the fields were paved over like roads. On the roads were airplanes so large I could not believe they could fly. Soon, I knew, we would be on one of those planes. I had looked up at the planes in the sky from the rice paddies. From such a distance how small they had seemed! Now we would be up in the sky looking down. Everything we were leaving behind would grow small, but not so small that we would ever forget it.

AFTERWORD

In recent months, prospects for the approximately 60,000 Vietnamese boat people who have made the perilous journey to Hong Kong have taken a turn for the worse. Unlike Mai and Kim and their families, the refugees now in the camps have almost no chance of coming to America or even of remaining in detention in Hong Kong. At present, they are undergoing a screening process to determine whether they are economic or political refugees. Most, designated as economic refugees, will be returned to Vietnam against their will.